LOVE SPELL

Jennifer's Story

REIGN ATKINS

For Isabella.

PROLOGUE

Richmont, 1533

You can't have love without tragedy. Try as you might, but there is no disproving the fact that all great loves either stem from disaster or end in heartbreak. No matter how riveting and passionate the journey may be.

Take the Morris Curse for instance.

Interchangeably known as the Morris-Colby Curse for it wasn't only the Morris witches that were affected.

While the line of Morris Witches dates back further than the 1500's, it was a young, scrappy, and powerful Morris Witch who gave her whole heart, only to be scorned in the process.

That woman was Rose Morris. Rose was as beautiful as she was powerful, and she befriended a girl by the name of Hayami Sen.

When Rose was sixteen, she had started courting the boy that her parents had arranged for her to marry. Armando Colby.

But unlike many arranged marriages which focused solely on lands and dowries, the love between Rose and Armando was true. Perfect. Pure.

But Rose was unaware of the feelings her new friend, Hayami, had for Armando.

It wasn't until the night before their wedding, when Rose snuck out of her home in the dead of night and arrived at the stables of the Colby Estate, that she bore witness to the very event that would spark a curse which would span for generations.

It was there, at the stables that Rose bore witness to Hayami and Armando kissing.

Brokenhearted, Rose did not wait to hear Armando's explanation.

That explanation Hayami had tried numerous times to steal his affections, but Armando's heart had always belonged to Rose.

That moment in the stables had only ever been a one-sided kiss and when Armando had seen the horror on Rose's face, he had chased after her and even called out.

Instead of listening, Rose, being as stubborn and stricken with grief, poured her emotions into a spell which tied Armando Colby's soul to that of a wolf.

And she didn't stop there. Rose cursed the entire male Colby bloodline too. And for Hayami's treacherous ways, Rose forced Hayami to live forever with heartbreak and tied her soul to that of a cunning and deceitful fox.

But anybody who understands magic knows that a spell so great would come back to Rose tenfold. And that spell did just that.

Rose did fall in love with another man and then she had a daughter. Though soon after she fell pregnant, her new love died. And so, the curse expanded throughout the Morris bloodline. Each Morris woman who bore a child only ever bore a daughter. Never a son.

And every man they loved and who loved them in return would meet an untimely death.

Throughout generations the Morris Curse evolved. And soon, a Morris Charm was born alongside it. That charm was a lure that would make Morris women irresistible to any potential lover. But still, death was the fate of all who truly loved them. Gradually, the news of the Morris Curse spread amongst the non-mortals and has only ever strengthened over time forcing these women to become the strongest and most powerful line of witches to have lived.

To a wolf, particularly from the Colby bloodline, the very scent of a Morris Witch reminds them of lavender, which is the flower that Armando Colby gave to Rose when they were children.

While many speculate the only way to break the curse would be for a Morris witch to give birth to a Colby child, there has been no success in that endeavor. Still, the curse doesn't stop the complicated emotions that continue to plague generation after generation of Morris Witches and Colby sons.

And what of Hayami Sen?

...Well, she's still around.

ONE

Richmont, 2006

I t was a warm Tuesday morning as seventeen-year-old Jennifer Morris ate her oatmeal, with her attention drawn to the television in the kitchen. Pushing her auburn hair from her face, Jennifer tried to get a better look at the body, as the officers covered it in a black sheet and the blond news reporter narrated the scene. "The body of a fifteen-year-old Richmont High School student washed up on the beach this morning with no physical signs of abuse.

While investigators are ruling her death as…" the reporter's voice came to an abrupt halt as the screen went black.

Annoyed, Jennifer turned her green eyes to her hippy-witch of a mother, who's hand was still pointed at the television, minus the remote control.

"Hey, I was watching that!" Jennifer whined.

"Well, now you're not," Marian replied. "That's the third murder this week. If we're not careful they'll turn this whole ordeal into a modern-day witch hunt and come knocking at our door."

Jennifer rolled her eyes and turned her focus back to the blank television screen, tempted to switch it back on with her own powers.

Even though their large house had retained its charm since it was first established as Morris Manor in the 15th century, she had managed to convince her mother to keep with the times and invest in modern technology. The televisions in the kitchen and the living room were pure examples of the case. As was her phone and laptop.

"Actually, mom," Jennifer argued. "They believe those murders were nothing more than teen suicides. Drug overdoses, even."

"Drug overdoses? Pfft! All that science is going to ruin your aptitude for magic. You know damn well it wasn't a drug overdose, there's a lot more out there than just..." As Marian continued, Jennifer sent a text on her phone and continued to eat her breakfast.

Yes, there was more out there than science. There were witches, werewolves, vampires, and so much more. Every paranormal tale the mortals believed to be works of fiction were all true. But of course, the mortals had no idea... unless they happened to find themselves at the mercy of one. And in that case, they probably wouldn't live to tell the tale.

How did Jennifer know?

Well, she was a non-mortal. A Morris Witch, in fact. Just as Marian was a Morris Witch. Just as every Morris woman of their lineage before them had been too. Their long lineage dated back since before the 12th century and while being a Morris Witch had its perks, it also had its curses.

For one thing, the men they loved, never lasted. Whether they be non-mortal or mortal alike.

That included the men that fathered their children. Many of them generally met a bitter end.

It was as if to be loved by a Morris Witch, also meant to be cursed by them. Another issue that Jennifer had with being a witch was that while Marian made a living out of making simple spells and seances for the locals, Jennifer was bound to keep her identity a secret. Sure, she could cause one person to fall in love with her and make another wish they had never been born. Jennifer could even converse with the dead. But if she told a single mortal soul, it could potentially change not only the town's views on she and her mother, but the entire mortal perception of the existence of non-mortals.

There had only ever been one person to whom Jennifer had revealed her truth. And that was *Sebastian Colby*.

Catching the tail-end of Marian's overly rehearsed lecture, Jennifer relayed the words she had heard time and time again with her mouth filled with oatmeal.

"I mustn't lose sight of who I am and that I'm different to the mortals. Come on, mom. I know. Besides, doesn't your job risk them bringing the old-fashioned witch hunt to our house, as it is?"

"Don't talk with your mouthful. And for your information, I offer my customers simple remedies and hope. You mustn't mix them up. Besides, aren't you late for school?"

Jennifer glanced at her phone. 9:17am.

"Oh crap!" She darted from the chair, grabbed her backpack, kissed her mother on the cheek and headed towards the door, leaving her empty bowl on the table. She had already missed the school bus... Again. But that wasn't a problem, for Jennifer had other plans that day.

"I can always drive..." Before Marian could finish her sentence, Jennifer raised her hand.

"Ah, no. We're not doing that again." But as she went to leave, her mother pointed to her filthy bowl.

"Uh uh, Jennifer! I'm not your housekeeper."

On Jennifer's gestures, the bowl rose up into the air and spun around, cleaning itself. Then, with a flick of her wrist, it flung into the opened cupboard with the others. "Better?"

"Much. I love you, Jennifer."

With a quick over-the-shoulder "love you too" Jennifer raced out the door and into the warm sun.

As she trailed the dirt path of Marian's extravagant herb garden, which smelled strongly of rosemary that morning, Jennifer pulled out her phone and got to texting. She merely had to wait a few minutes before a grey sedan pulled up alongside her. After checking to see that her mother wasn't watching, Jennifer climbed into the passenger side. For a seventeen-year-old, Aisha Prescott reminded Jennifer of an African queen.

Her hair was always kept back, styled in tight black braids, and she wore black eyeliner in the same way the Ancient Egyptians used to.

"Are you ready?" Aisha asked the moment Jennifer buckled in her seatbelt.

"Of course, I am. Now let's go, before my mom catches us heading in the wrong direction."

Aisha accelerated down the road, with them both equally excited to get to their destination.

✳✳✳

Jennifer and Aisha left the restrooms of the Underground club dressed very differently from how they had first looked when Jennifer had left the house. While Aisha wore a tight black dress, Jennifer was now in a short purple dress and a black leather jacket. Amongst the sea of ravers dancing to the live rock band, *Sex Angels,* the girls fitted in perfectly. Nobody would've guessed that they were supposed to be sitting in a high school classroom and thanks to Jennifer's powers, nobody would question their absence either. The band consisted of a very attractive lead singer with cropped dark hair, blue eyes, and a soulful voice.

A lead guitarist, who looked very similar to the vocalist, only with short, wavey hair with a lock that fell over his eye as he played.

A blond female drummer and a scrawny, blond male keyboardist. They were dressed in faded, black T-shirts, jeans and their very aura smelled of seduction mixed with regret. While their music possessed a heavy rock'n'roll theme, their songs were deep and emotional. It was intoxicating. Dangerous. *Perfect.*

The music ignited something in Jennifer which told her that magic was certainly at play.

While Aisha danced to the rhythm, Jennifer's eyes fell to the dark-haired, blue-eyed guitarist lost in his guitar solo. She could feel that he wasn't mortal. Nor was he a witch, vampire, or wolf. But he was... *something.* Tempted to use her powers to find out what, Jennifer focused all her attention on him, just as Aisha pulled her away. "Hey girl. I'm thirsty. Let's go drink."

With her concentration broken, Jennifer came to realize her own thirst... And not just for the lead guitarist. She followed Aisha towards the bar, where her friend ordered two cocktails, while doing her best to appear older than she really was.

Just as Jennifer was sure the blond bartender would buy Aisha's act an almost hypnotic masculine voice broke in overtop. "Make them virgin cocktails and I'll pay for them myself."

Tongue in cheek, Jennifer turned to the lead guitarist who had spoken. He barely looked much older than them. "Virgin cocktails? Are you kidding me?"

"Well, you don't exactly look twenty-one. You don't want the bartender to lose her license, do you?" His remark was confident. Too confident.

Jennifer had met many guys like him in the past. But none of them were immune to the Morris charm. She exchanged looks with Aisha to hear her friend's opinion.

"Hey, if he's buying, I don't care what we drink." True Aisha fashion.

Swapping her irritation for charm, Jennifer smiled at the guy.

"Alright, deal. Two virgin cocktails and you're buying." He nodded at the bartender then turned back to Jennifer.

"The name's Emerick."

"Jennifer. What kind of name is Emerick?"

"Old fashioned name. Shouldn't you be at school? You don't exactly look old enough to..."

"...I'll take that as a compliment. Tell me more about you."

A surprised smile crossed Emerick's lips but instead of answering, he nodded towards the bartender. "Your drinks."

As the girls took their drinks, Aisha whispered under her breath, "Get him to introduce me to the singer."

Her question brought their attention to the band's lead vocalist, who was taking a mouthful of water beside the stage. With a readied smile, Jennifer turned back to Emerick.

"So, who's your singer?"

"Are you talking about Ambrose?"

Jennifer shrugged and waited for Emerick to go on. "He's my brother. But before you get any ideas, let me give you some advice. Stay as far away from him as you can."

"Ooh, forbidden fruit," Aisha said. "Even better."

"I'm sure he's not that bad," Jennifer added.

But Emerick shook his head. "I'm serious. He eats up high school girls like you for breakfast."

"We never said we were in high school," Jennifer argued.

"You didn't have to. I've seen your type before. You come in here wearing short dresses wanting to sleep with the band and then when things go south, which they normally do, you..."

"...Woah, hey!" Aisha cut in. "I don't expect to bring him home to my parents I just want..."

"...Alright, we'll take your word," Jennifer interjected. "We'll stay away from him."

"Speak for yourself," Aisha grumbled. Without another word, she took off towards the vocalist.

With a quick curse under her breath, Jennifer stormed through the crowd after her best friend, reaching her just as Aisha was introducing herself to the slightly older version of Emerick.

"Hi, you have a really great voice," Aisha said, mustering her charm.

"Yeah? You think so?"

"I really do. I mean, it's so soulful, not like all the other artists you hear out there."

"Thanks. The name's Ambrose."

"Aisha."

Jennifer took in the man's demeanor and immediately picked up on the same aura that she had sensed with his brother. The guys were perfectly attractive, and they literally breathed danger. But it wasn't the everyday, typical bad boy persona. Her instincts told her the exact same thing that Emerick had said moments ago. To stay right away from him. As Ambrose noticed Jennifer standing behind Aisha, his crystal eyes lit up.

"And what was your name?"

Before Jennifer could think up a fake name, Aisha wrapped her arm around her shoulder and pulled her in tight. "Oh, this is my girl, Jennifer."

"Jennifer, huh? Are you from around here?" Jennifer pulled out of Aisha's arm and turned her full focus onto her friend.

"Aisha, did you forget? We have that *meeting* at the office to get to?"

"What are you talking about? We haven't got..."
But as Jennifer looked her squarely in the eyes
mentally pleading that she go with it, Aisha's
realization hit hard.

"Oh! *That* meeting."

"So, can we go, now?"

"We don't need to. I took care of it." Jennifer
could've slapped Aisha.

As much as she wanted to leave what felt like the
dankest pits of a demon's lair, she was stuck in the
very thick of it, uncomfortably watching Aisha flirt
with Ambrose. Jennifer thought back to a spell her
mother had taught her years ago. *'Friend or foe'.*

Unfortunately, that spell was only useful when
determining one's agenda. But just maybe she could
adjust it a little. Jennifer took a breath, prepared the
words in her mind, and went to chant just as her
focus was interrupted by the feeling of a hand on
her back. She turned to see Emerick beside her.

"Ambrose, don't we need to be back on stage in five? We should really leave these young ladies alone."

"Oh, right. Will I see you again?" Ambrose asked.

Giving Aisha no chance to respond, Jennifer pulled her away, cutting their conversation entirely. "Maybe you will, maybe you won't," Jennifer said. "We were literally passing through town. Only came here on a business trip... You know how it is."

With her friend fighting hard against her non-mortal strength, Jennifer dragged Aisha towards the exits where they stopped to compose themselves.

"Seriously, Jennifer? How could you cockblock me like that?"

"I'm sorry but I was doing you a favor."

"Girl, you got some real strength there. And how are you doing me a favor? You're supposed to be my wing-girl."

"I *am* being your wing-girl. It's my job to look out for you. Ambrose felt like bad news."

"And that's what makes him sexy. You know bad boys are my jam." That was true. Aisha really did have a thing for bad boys. But Ambrose was beyond bad boy material. Jennifer glanced over at Emerick.

He, Ambrose, and the rest of the band were preparing for their next song. Jennifer turned back to Aisha, needing to be honest with her. Not too honest, but honest just the same. "Aisha, I'm not talking about your typical 'skipping class to do drugs' bad boy, I'm talking about something much worse."

"Like jailtime bad boy?" Her excitement was obvious.

"Worse."

"What's worse than jail time bad boy?"

"I'm talking about an actual monster." Thanks to the serious look of surprise, Jennifer felt like she was getting through to her.

That was until Aisha burst into laughter.

"Oh my god, you're so funny."

Knowing that Aisha was bound to return to Ambrose after their next song, Jennifer made a drastic, though desperate move.

In mere seconds, Aisha's phone rang. Her eyes went wide with shock... Unsurprisingly, Jennifer's phone rang too.

Thanks to Jennifer's powers, their school and parents had all learned that they had cut class.

But at least the trouble they'd be in with their parents couldn't amount to the trouble they'd be in if they had stayed.

TWO

J ust after three in the afternoon, Jennifer approached her front door, mentally preparing herself for the lecture she was yet to receive from her mother. She hesitated as she reached for the old, brass doorknob. But before Jennifer could make contact, the large wooden door opened on its own. Marian was nowhere to be seen.

With a groan, Jennifer stepped into the living room and looked around.

"Mom? Are you home?" No answer.

Clearly, Marian was giving her the silent treatment for skipping class and would most likely be in her summoning room.

Jennifer wondered what punishment Marian had cooked up this time. Scrubbing the cauldron by hand, maybe? Possibly even dusting every shelf in the old house. Ready to take her lashings, Jennifer tiptoed up the stairs, headed for the room that Marian spent most of her time.

Once she had reached the top floor, Jennifer peered towards the slightly opened door at the end of the hallway, where she could hear her mother speaking softly. Assuming she was chanting a spell, Jennifer prepared to turn on her heels and head back down the steps, until she heard Marian's voice call out to her. "Jennifer, get in here."

With a quick curse under her breath, Jennifer picked up her pace, until she reached the door to her mother's summoning room.

Cautiously, she pushed it open.

The summoning room was by far, the smallest room in the entire house. But it did its job.

Every shelf was filled with numerous items that could be used in spells, potions, readings, and rituals. Large black curtains concealed the wide windows to the world outside.

In the corner by the door was a medium-sized black cauldron which sat on a shelf, surrounded by herbs. A small round table with one wooden stool for Marian to sit on, and two stools across the table for her guests to sit, took up the space in the middle. And on that table sat the infamous leatherbound Morris Witch spell book and a brightly lit crystal ball. Without skipping a breath, Jennifer began her apology. "Mom, I'm so sorry I skipped school. There was this band and Aisha and I wanted to go and…" Stopping mid-speech, Jennifer took in the sight of the visitor who sat opposite Marian. *Emerick.*

"I believe I need no introduction," Marian said, getting to her feet and motioning towards him.

"No, mom," Jennifer replied, solemn.

"Good. Because I don't know how many times, I need to tell you that I will not condone lying in this house. Do I make myself clear?"

"Yes, mom."

Jennifer waited for the lecture of skipping class. But it didn't come.

Instead, a delightful smile spread across Marian's face as she rubbed her hands together. "Now, Jennifer. Emerick is new to town. He came to me in need of a reading, and we got to talking. Can you believe it? He's staying at that old Barrett Manor. The very place is riddled with dark magic. So, I invited him to stay here, with us. And it will be your duty to show him around Richmont. Is that clear?"

"Wait, what?"

"Oh, you heard me. It's lonely being a non-mortal in this town. He will accompany you to school and you will help him settle in. Now, don't you have homework to do? Go and do it."

Jennifer exchanged a highly confused glance with Emerick before mouthing her confusion to her mother. "But I skipped school. Aren't you going to punish me for that?"

"Oh no, Jennifer. And do you want to know why?" Without giving her the chance to respond, Marian answered her own question. "Because you know you made a mistake and you fixed it with magic. And honestly, to our kind having our children fix their own mistakes by magic is all one can ever really ask for."

Jennifer was perplexed on how she had just escaped serious trouble. If she had been a mortal she would've been grounded for life.

But instead, she had been given the task of showing the very attractive new guy around town.

At that very thought, Jennifer's look of confusion changed into a subtle look of excitement.

With a quick, "thanks mom," she turned on her heels and left the room, headed for downstairs.

✳ ✳ ✳

After roughly ten minutes of essay typing, Jennifer looked up to see Emerick join her at the table with his own computer.

"I just knew you couldn't get enough of me," she said.

"Aren't you confident?" Emerick replied. "But no. I came here for an entirely different reason."

"Yeah, to see my mother. I bet."

"Joke all you like, but it's the truth. Your mother is a Morris witch, so I asked her to help me figure out who is responsible for a string of murders across the state."

Jennifer's blood grew cold. How had she not seen it before? Emerick must've been a hunter.

A powerful non-mortal who could cloak their identities from other non-mortals for the sheer duty of hunting and killing. "You're a hunter, then? Look, we've cooperated with you. Please, don't hurt…"

"…Relax. I'm not a hunter. Besides, if I was, do you really think I could've stepped past your mother's protection spells? But if you must know that girl that washed up on the shore this morning was an old friend of mine and it's my duty to find out who killed her."

Jennifer thought back to that morning's news report. So, her mother was right. The girl's death had been carried out by a non-mortal.

Frustrated, Jennifer slumped back into her chair. While having non-mortals in Richmont wasn't uncommon, murders being carried out by non-mortals certainly was.

For the innocent witches, wolves, vampires, and other beings who called Richmont their home, this new cause of events was bound to attract the attention of the public as well as bring the hunters to their door. It was no wonder, Marian had requested Emerick to stay with them, at least she could help solve the case and keep a watchful eye on him at the same time. But what about his brother?

"Is Ambrose going to be staying with us too?" Jennifer asked.

Emerick leaned back in his chair and turned his focus to the news article on his computer. "Unlikely. He's a real fan of Barrett Manor."

"A true vampire, huh?"

A surprised chuckle escaped Emerick's lips. "Aren't you clever? You figured out my secret." His blatant sarcasm told her she couldn't be further from the truth with what he was.

"So, you're *not* a vampire? Then, what are you?"

"That's really none of your concern. Besides, don't you have schoolwork to do?"

Frustrated by his arrogance, Jennifer scoffed. How could he just shut her down like that? And not once, but twice in one day.

"Fine. Have it your way," she said and without another word, Jennifer picked up her laptop and took it to her room to study.

✳ ✳ ✳

Later that night, as Jennifer lay sprawled on her bed, messaging Aisha who had not only been grounded but had also had her car taken away for a whole month, she startled at a knock on her door. Knowing that her mother had gone out to a ritual celebration with her coven, she didn't need to concentrate too hard to figure out who it was.

"What do you want, Emerick?"

"Can I come in? I need your help."

Jennifer scanned her slightly untidy room. She'd only ever had one boy step past that threshold, and that had been Sebastian Colby. Now, she found herself in the uncomfortable feeling of not knowing how to act around a very handsome bedroom visitor. Clambering to sit cross-legged on her bed, Jennifer put down her phone and adopted a semi-casual tone. "Sure, make yourself at home."

On her response, Emerick wandered in, taking a seat by the desk. Judging by the look on his face, there was something serious on his mind. "Are you alright?" she asked.

"So, we've been following the murders for a while now and after travelling to six different towns, one thing is evident. The deaths are always on high school girls and there's never any signs of foul play or suicide. Nor do any drugs come up in their system."

"How do you know? I doubt the police will give you free reign to examine the bodies."

"Not me, Ambrose. When not playing with the band, he takes the role of a young Private Investigator. He's good at what he does."

"Yet, you still lure girls away from him like he's some kind of monster."

Taking in her words, Emerick lowered his tone. "To some he is. It's a part of what we are and what we do. And for that, it's just best if girls don't get attached. You see, we're cursed to not fall in love with anybody nor have anybody fall in love with us. That poses a danger for high school mortals. But while it's in their best interest to listen, they see it as a supernatural teen romance and just can't help but get involved."

Jennifer giggled. "Are you sure you're not a vampire? I've read so many books that started out just this way."

"Positive. And I know what you're thinking. Ambrose isn't responsible for the deaths. In fact, I think whoever is doing it, is hunting us."

Jennifer considered his words. It was an eerie thought. "Why tell me?"

"Because I need your help figuring out who the killer is. You're the perfect age and you and your friend could be prime targets."

"Prime targets?"

"Don't take this the wrong way, but you're very pretty and clearly your friend has a real thirst for danger. If you help me, we may be able to stop whoever it is before anybody else gets hurt."

While Jennifer had grown quite used to boys complimenting her, there was something highly flattering about Emerick calling her pretty that made her blush. But the thought of her friends finding themselves the next target of some psychopath was chilling.

"Alright, I'll help. What do you need me to do?"

At her agreement, Emerick's blue eyes twinkled, making him appear more attractive than ever. Whatever curse prevented him from getting close to anybody, it must've been severe.

✳✳✳

The next morning was Wednesday and as Jennifer stepped aboard the school bus, all eyes diverted to the attractive new student that had accompanied her. While Jennifer was quite used to turning heads thanks to the Morris charm, she wasn't at all used to the attention being diverted away from her. Still, she trailed rows until she reached her seat beside Aisha, leaving Emerick to sit behind them. Upon seeing the new student Aisha's eyes grew wide with excitement. "Why didn't you tell me he was staying with you?"

Jennifer shrugged. "I didn't know until last night when my mom sprung it on me. Apparently, he's an old family friend."

"What about his brother? Is he staying with you too?"

"No, he prefers to do his own thing."

As Aisha turned her smile forward, she mouthed the word, 'lucky' under her breath.

Before Jennifer could exchange glances with Emerick, Richmont's own Asian-American head cheerleader, Chelsea Lee and her brunette sidekick, Daniella De La Cruz turned back from the seat in front. Despite being in the same social group, Jennifer and Chelsea had an unspoken rivalry, and had done so since the day they had first met.

"Ooh, new guy looks delicious. What's his deal?" Chelsea asked, not caring that Emerick could hear her.

"No deal. He's just staying with my mom and I for a little..." before Jennifer could finish, Chelsea moved to sit beside Emerick.

"Let's just hope she doesn't lay eyes on Ambrose," Aisha said under her breath.

As Jennifer silently agreed, she turned her focus to Daniella who was surprisingly quiet that morning. "Are you alright?"

Daniella nodded, but the look in her brown eyes told a whole other story.

"Can we chat in private when we get off the bus?" Daniella asked, almost in a whisper.

"Of course."

Just as Jennifer said those words, the bus came to an immediate stop. They had arrived at Richmont High School. Richmont High was very big and very old. In fact, in the early eighteenth century, it had been a boarding school when a fire had broken out in the west wing.

While mortals saw it as just a school with its urban legends, to Jennifer, it was something else.

Ghosts loomed the halls and sat silent in classrooms as if they were still living and breathing students. And while Jennifer could never voice what she saw to anybody, it didn't stop her from seeing them. As Jennifer stepped off the bus in between Daniella and Aisha, she sent a sympathetic look at Emerick who was politely dismissing Chelsea's desperate attempts at a date.

Remembering, what he had said about being cursed, Jennifer silently wished him all the luck because the girl could never to take 'no' for an answer. Suddenly, Daniella grabbed her hand, forcing Jennifer to turn to see Richmont High's Sebastian Colby dressed in his blue and white football uniform, surrounded by the rest of his team.

Of course, he was the center of attention. He was ultimately handsome. His dark hair adopted an untamable wave. His eyes were brown but possessed amber streaks. And he was very muscular for a guy their age. It was no wonder he was Richmont's star quarter back and his team's alpha. People rarely crossed him. Unless they were Jennifer, of course. Thanks to a very long list of reasons mostly related to the Morris-Colby curse he and Jennifer would always be connected whether they were together or not. Sebastian and Jennifer had known one another their whole lives. Their parents had known each other through their high school days... and their parents knew each other before that. But Jennifer and Sebastian, well, their relationship had always been complicated.

In grade school, Sebastian had made a vow that they would get married when they grew up. Then they dated when they were twelve. And then again when they were fifteen. He had been Jennifer's first and vice versa. But then high school got in the way and Sebastian dated more girls than Jennifer could count, and Jennifer moved on.

Well, she tried...

While Marian had been their greatest champion, the woman also believed that the answer to ending the Morris-Colby curse lied within Jennifer and Sebastian. But after having known Sebastian inside and out their entire lives, Jennifer's belief in the wolf part of the curse had subsided a very long time ago. Currently, Daniella and Sebastian had been dating off and on for the past year and judging by Daniella's current need to ignore him, it was obvious that Sebastian was her problem.

Taking the hint, Jennifer guided Daniella and the rest of their friends out of Sebastian's path, leaving the guy completely puzzled as he turned to face them. After they were out of Sebastian's earshot,

Jennifer addressed Daniella. "Okay spill. Why did we just avoid your boyfriend?"

Daniella peered over at Aisha, Emerick, and Chelsea who were all standing only a few feet away. "Can we talk in private, please, Jennifer?"

"It's alright. Go," Aisha said.

Jennifer caught the attention of Emerick who looked like a prisoner to Chelsea's overly friendly behavior. Unfortunately, he'd need to handle Chelsea himself, while Jennifer headed to the girls' restrooms with Daniella. After checking every stall in the bathroom to ensure they had the privacy they needed, Jennifer joined the eerily pale Daniella at the sinks.

"Are you okay?" she asked, as the girl flushed her face with cold water.

Daniella nodded. But then her nod turned into a complete shake of the head.

"No, I'm not. I really need to tell you something. Please, don't be mad at me."

"Mad at you? How could I be mad at you?"

"You know, you and Sebastian have a... complicated history."

Jennifer chuckled. But it was a false chuckle primarily for her friend's benefit. The last thing Jennifer wanted was to come between Daniella and Sebastian.

"Daniella, it's fine. Sebastian and I haven't been together in so long. You're good."

"Really? Because you really need to keep this a secret. Don't even tell Aisha or Chelsea. Do you swear?"

"Of course, I swear. What's going on?"

Daniella started pacing. And as she paced, the words fell from her lips, involuntarily.

"My parents are seriously going to kill me."

"Kill you? What for? Why?"

Daniella stopped in front of Jennifer. Her face was drenched in terror. "Jennifer, I'm... I'm pregnant with Sebastian's baby. I need you to take me to your mom. I need her help."

THREE

Of all the things Jennifer had predicted to happen that morning, having Daniella reveal that she was pregnant with Sebastian's child, would've never been on that list.

Yet, there she was. And to make matters worse, Daniella was requesting the help of Marian, which merely pointed to the fact that she knew Jennifer's secret. Or did she?

"Why do you need my mom's help?" Jennifer asked.

"I need an herbal remedy. Something that can help me get rid of this thing. Please, Jennifer. My parents can't find out."

"Are you sure that's what you want? I mean, I can talk to my mother but you're talking about..."

"...I don't know if it's what I want. But what other option do I have?"

Over a hundred answers of what Daniella could do flashed through Jennifer's mind. But ultimately, it wasn't Jennifer's decision. So, she asked the one question that did come to mind.

"Does Sebastian know?"

"Not yet. But if word gets out, he'll find out soon enough." Caught between a rock and a hard place, Jennifer messaged Aisha, *'Can you cover for us? I'll be back before lunch,'* then led Daniella out of the restrooms. Once they reached the corridor, they found themselves standing face to face with Emerick. Somehow, he had managed to lose Chelsea. "Is everything alright?" he asked.

"It's fine, Emerick... I just need to take Daniella..." Jennifer paused midsentence to witness the horrible look of nausea that washed over Daniella right before she vomited all over their shoes with what looked to be bright red blood. Students all around reacted as if Daniella was the star character from an exorcism movie.

"Oh, my goddess!" Jennifer cried in wide-eyed horror. "We need to take her to my mom, right now!"

"On it!" Emerick said, lifting Daniella into his arms as Jennifer led him to the exits.

In seconds they were rushing through the school grounds, towards the parking lot with Daniella heaving up blood, uncontrollably.

In that moment, Jennifer wondered what the universe's punishment would be if she were to perform a large teleportation spell on all three of them. Unfortunately, the risk would be too high. They had no choice but to borrow a car.

Before she could decide on the car that they would borrow, Jennifer bumped hard into Sebastian Colby. "Morris, what's going on? What's wrong with Daniella?"

"Not the time, Colby!" Jennifer said, trying to bypass the quarterback. "We're taking her to my mom."

"Your mom? We need to take her to the damn hospital!"

"She's vomiting blood. Trust me, my mother's the best person to handle this."

Merely a second ticked by and Sebastian agreed. He held up his keys and rushed to the side door of the red jaguar sitting in the parking lot.

"We'll take mine."

As Jennifer climbed into the backseat ready to take Daniella from Emerick, Sebastian traded Emerick the keys for Daniella.

"Whatever your name is, don't crash it."

"You can't come with us," Jennifer told Sebastian as he climbed in the back of the car with Daniella.

"Over my dead body, Morris! There's no way in hell am I staying here."

But before they could continue their argument, Emerick sped out of the parking lot and down the road with some impressive driving skills.

As Daniella kept vomiting blood, Jennifer picked up an old blue shirt and noticed Sebastian looking a little queasy.

"What's the matter, Colby?" she asked, bringing the shirt to Daniella's mouth. "Blood never made you squeamish before."

"Let's just say," Sebastian said as his eyes flickered yellow, "A lot has changed in the past year." Jennifer's crippled skepticism of the wolf curse was replaced with a sudden fear and while she had never seen a wolf transformation before, something told her that she could potentially be seeing one very soon if Emerick didn't make it to her place in time.

"Oh, not now! Why didn't you tell me sooner?"

"And how do you expect that conversation to have gone? Our parents were right, I am a wolf. Will you ever forgive me for doubting you?"

"It would've been so much better than the possibility of you turning into one and killing us all while we're trying to help your girlfriend. Besides, I thought wolves only turned during full moons."

To avoid the sight of the blood that poured from Daniella's mouth, Sebastian turned his gaze to the window. "Full grown wolves, yeah... But for teenaged wolves who are just getting used to it... The scent of blood can send our bodies into hyper... hyperdrive."

"Oh, goddess!" Jennifer groaned at the sight of black fur growing at his neck. "Emerick, step on it!"

"I'm going as fast as I can," Emerick called back. "Oh, shit! The Sheriff's on our tail."

"What?!" Jennifer diverted her eyes from the bloody scene to look through the rear window. Sure enough, they were being trailed by Sheriff Mike, who sounded his alarm.

"Let me out!" Sebastian cried.

"The Sheriff wants us to pull over," Emerick said.

Sebastian's spine contorted in an inhumanly manner. "Just do it. Pull over!" he snapped.

"No, don't!" Jennifer cried. "My mom can help us."

"We don't have time! I'm turning now," Sebastian said.

"You need to do something, Jennifer!" Emerick broke in.

"Like what?"

"Just do… owwwww… something, Morris! Now!" A gut-wrenching howl came from Sebastian as he attempted to speak.

"I'm pulling over," Emerick said.

As the car pulled to the side, Jennifer knew that she was the only person who could do anything to save them from their situation.

As much as she hated her powers, the fear of Daniella vomiting up blood, Sebastian turning into a wolf and Sheriff Mike about to lock them away for speeding frightened her.

"Okay, PAUSE!" she yelled.

The moment she mouthed the word, time came to a standstill. Daniella stopped mid-heave. Sebastian's transformation didn't stop but slowed down to half pace. He now resembled some creepy half human, half wolf hybrid. Jennifer looked to Sheriff Mike who sat frozen in his car next to Deputy Olivia Henderson.

Jennifer looked to Emerick. He hadn't stopped or even slowed down at all. Which was strange, because while her powers were weak against non-mortals, they at least had some effect on them. "Emerick. Why aren't you frozen?"

"Now's not the time. We need to do something."

"Oh, uh… Right."

Jennifer did the only thing she could do.

She closed her eyes and mentally sent a message to her mom explaining their current predicament.

When her eyes finally opened, she knew what she needed to do. But whether it would work or not, was a whole other story.

"Emerick, I need you to get ready to distract Sheriff Mike. Leave Sebastian and Daniella to me."

"Are you sure?"

"No, but my mother will be here soon. Just don't leave until time goes back to normal. I don't want to freak them out."

Emerick unbuckled his seatbelt and turned back to her. "Okay. Good luck."

Jennifer brought her hand to Sebastian's hand which now resembled a dark paw. She hesitated before making contact.

A deep growl echoed from his doglike mouth and his eyes watched her, hesitant. With her hand to his paw, Jennifer began to chant.

"*Reverse transmutatio. Transmutatio reverse. Reverse transmutatio.*"

She could hear the slow cracking of bones as Sebastian's features morphed back into their original human shape.

It happened slowly and while she could barely imagine the pain he must've been enduring, there was nothing more she could do.

Soon enough, Sebastian was entirely back to human form, though still half-frozen. Jennifer turned to Emerick.

"Alright, he's good. I'm going to put time back to normal and clean up Daniella. Now go."

As Jennifer mentally pressed play to time, Emerick climbed out of the car to meet with the Sheriff, while Daniella got back to vomiting. Examining himself, Sebastian voiced his surprise, "Wow, Morris. What the hell did you just do?"

"I reversed your transformation."

"How the..."

"...It'll only hold off if we can clean up Daniella." Jennifer turned her attention back to the girl and whispered in her ear.

"Nausea begone. Now rest." On her command, Daniella stopped vomiting and passed out against the back of the seat. But Jennifer wasn't finished.

With a quick wave of her hand, the mess of blood that surrounded them dissipated, bringing the car back to its pristine state.

"Damn, Morris. I should pay you to clean my room."

"Very funny. I wouldn't step foot back in that minefield if you paid me. Now, look natural."

Sebastian rolled down his window just as Sheriff Mike approached, peering into the car to address them. "Hey Sheriff. Fine morning, huh?" Sebastian said.

"Miss Morris. MR Colby. Shouldn't you all be at school? What's wrong with her?"

The Sheriff motioned towards Daniella who was passed out on Jennifer's shoulder.

"It's all good," Sebastian said, casually.

"Daniella came to school with a bad headache this morning and Jennifer said her mom has the perfect remedy. We all have this big test later, so we thought we'd give it a shot."

"And neither of you thought of visiting the school nurse?"

"We wanted the non-drowsy sort," Jennifer improvised. "You know that lavender one you tried, last Halloween?" She was referring to a special herbal tea that Marian had given to the Sheriff the night he had been attacked by a poltergeist.

It had not only helped with the pain from being crushed by an invisible force, but also the mental trauma that had come with it.

As a mortal town Sheriff dealing with the often-unexplainable events in Richmont, he was a frequent customer in the Morris household. And was fortunately sworn to secrecy.

"Ah yes," Sheriff Mike said, turning to Emerick who was now standing beside him. "Strong stuff, that tea. Bitter, but strong. Oh, there's your mother now." On those words, Jennifer, Sebastian, and Emerick all looked to the brown range rover that had pulled up in front of them. Sure enough, her mother was rushing towards the Sheriff with a silver flask in her hand.

"Step aside, Sheriff. This girl is in desperate need of one of my teas," Marian said, pushing past him to hand Jennifer the flask. "Oh, look at the poor dear. She's passed out. You really should've seen me much sooner, Jennifer."

"I'm sorry, mom, but we came as fast as we could," Jennifer said, feeding the warm tea to Daniella who had just started to wake up.

As she did, Marian turned to the Sheriff and mustered her Morris charm to steal the attention. "I'm truly sorry, Mike. I understand that you were only doing your job but..."

"...They were speeding, Miss Morris," Sheriff Mike said, sternly. "And not just ten miles over the speed limit, but double."

"Double the speed limit? Oh, my goddess. Well, it was an emergency."

"That's no…" before the Sheriff could continue, Marian placed her hand on his shoulder and delivered her sweetest smile. "I don't know how I never realized just how blue your eyes are, Sheriff. How long has it been since Margaret left? Three years?"

As Marian continued to charm the man, Emerick climbed into the front seat and exchanged confused looks with Jennifer.

"Damn Morris charm," Sebastian chuckled under his breath. "Works every time."

"I take it you've been fooled before?" Emerick asked.

"I'm a Colby. We're the reason it exists. Besides, I've known Jennifer since we were kids. That charm has plagued me my whole life. So, yeah, being fooled by it comes with the territory."

Brushing off how easily Sebastian could speak so openly about her annoyed Jennifer enough to turn her attention entirely on Daniella.

The tea in the flask had certainly brought some color back to her face. "Look, guys! She's looking better."

"Hey, Daniella," Sebastian spoke softly, pulling her into his arms. "You gave us a big scare. Are you alright?" With Daniella nuzzling into Sebastian, Jennifer looked to her mother who had succeeded in getting rid of the Sheriff.

"Thanks mom. That was close but did you really need to ask him out on a date?"

"I didn't need to, Jenny. I wanted to. There's a big difference." Marian's eyes landed on Sebastian and Daniella before growing wide with realization. "Oh dear, this will not do at all. When you told me she was vomiting blood, I didn't realize it was *that* severe!"

"Severe?" Sebastian cried. "What's the matter with her?"

"Don't play innocent, Sebastian. You should be proud to add a Colby cub to the pack. But I guess I always thought it would be a Morris-Colby hybrid. You know, a blessing to break the curse." While Marian continued to reveal the secret that Daniella had wanted kept private, Jennifer watched the hurricane of emotions storm through Sebastian's eyes.

"Oh, well. Get the girl into the car. I'll need to look her over at home. You do realize, Sebastian, that by planting your seed, you've doomed that mortal to a world of hell."

Silence filled the car due to the sympathy both Jennifer and Emerick felt for Sebastian, until Marian adopted a tone of authority and opened his door. "Come on, people. We don't have all day. Get her in my car, now!"

Sebastian climbed out of the car and with the help of Emerick, the two assisted Daniella into Marian's brown range rover.

After joining her mother, Jennifer voiced her frustration. "I can't believe you told Sebastian that Daniella was pregnant. She asked me to keep it a secret!"

"Don't be silly, Jenny. Sebastian is a wolf. I'm surprised he couldn't smell the child. But I meant what I said. That girl is a young mortal. Her body might not be strong enough to withstand the pregnancy."

"What do you mean?"

"Exactly what I said. Mortals are weak when it comes to paranormal pregnancies. Sebastian's mother would've never survived if it wasn't for my ambrosia tea. I'm just hoping the girl can stomach it." On those words, they were joined by Emerick and Sebastian.

"Do you think she'll be alright?" Emerick asked.

"No promises. But I love a challenge," Marian replied. "Now, the rest of you head back to school. I'll notify Jennifer when Daniella is feeling better." Without another word, Marian raced back to her car, leaving Jennifer with Sebastian and Emerick.

"So," Sebastian began. "I'm going to be a dad. Did you know about that, Jennifer?"

Jennifer bit down on her lip as Sebastian received his answer. "Why the hell didn't you tell me? Daniella and I… We were never supposed to… How could I have been so stupid? Goddammit!" To emphasize his point, Sebastian's fist slammed through the left rear window of his car. There was no doubt about it, the guy was pissed.

FOUR

As Jennifer and Emerick stood back on the side of the road watching Sebastian pour out his frustration on his car, the two spoke amongst themselves. "Is Richmont High always this eventful?" Emerick asked.

"Oh, there's always drama. Just, normally it isn't so… non-mortal related. We generally keep that on the down low."

"Like the ghosts in the halls that no mortal sees?"

"Precisely. Even Sebastian knows to keep the wolf side of himself a secret. I'm really not looking forward to the conversation I'll be having with Daniella over the thought of her carrying a werewolf cub."

"Could be worse."

"How so?"

Emerick stared in silence for what felt like an eternity, almost as if he were attempting to read her mind forcing Jennifer to feel that same pull that his music had ignited at their concert.

That aura of dangerous seduction.

Was that the same pull that her victims felt when enslaved by the Morris charm? What was he and why was he immune to her powers?

Emerick turned his focus to Sebastian who was now sitting on the hood of his smashed car. "His soul calls out to you."

"His soul? What do you mean?"

"Call it one of my gifts, but I can read the souls of others. While Sebastian only ever dated Daniella as a distraction, he never got over you. He believes everything your mother said about the two of you being fated. The wolf in him is just as confused as the human in him."

Jennifer wanted to argue. How could he read souls? Furthermore, how could he claim that about Sebastian's soul? While those questions plagued her, they forced her to consider one question which was far more important than the rest.

Could he read *her* soul?

Jennifer approached Sebastian as one might approach a wounded beast.

"I'm sorry you had to find out that way, Sebastian," she said, brushing the glass away to take a seat beside him. "Daniella only told me while we were in the bathroom because she wanted me to take her to my mother. She was hoping for something that would get rid of it, but..."

"...Get rid of it?" as his voice encouraged her to clarify, his dark eyes peered at her like a rescue dog waiting for a new owner.

"Yeah. She's terrified of what her parents might do if they find out."

Understanding, Sebastian nodded. "It's gonna shock so many people. My parents included. They always thought... Well, I guess it doesn't matter anymore." His trailed silence only emphasized Jennifer's thoughts. But those thoughts had no place in the everchanging reality. She prepared her response, but he broke in before she could speak up. "I was actually going to break up with her."

"What did you just say?" she asked.

He nodded, as if to confirm what he had just said. "We've been dating off and on for a year because it's just so hard being with somebody that I don't love, when the one I do love is so far out of my reach."

"You're not... You're not talking about me, are you?"

"Of course, I am. Call it the Morris-Colby curse or whatever, but you're always on my mind and it's like I can sense you from a mile away. If you're scared, happy, sad. I feel it. Do you ever feel that way? About me?"

She'd be lying if she said she didn't. But he was living in dreams. He wasn't being realistic or thinking rationally.

Daniella was pregnant with his child. He had no right to say any of those things. "Sebastian... We can't keep looking to the past. We've been led to believe that we were meant to be together thanks to that curse. But Daniella's my friend and she's pregnant with your baby. That's life and we need to accept it whether we like it or not."

By his pause, it was evident to Jennifer that he didn't want to hear those words.

Alas, he sighed and nodded. "Damn Morris. There's that charm of yours. Just a surprise to see you use it for good."

Getting to her feet, Jennifer brought both her palms to the hood of the car. "As an olive branch for not telling you about Daniella and as an early baby shower gift, let me fix this. *Instaurabo!*"

Shards of glass flew through the air, piecing themselves and landing in the car's window frames, smoothing out perfectly. Even the dents in the vehicle disappeared. Sebastian got to his feet and pulled Jennifer into a hug, forcing her to breath in the scent of his musky aftershave and feel slammed by the overwhelming sensation of heartbreak.

Why the hell hadn't she gone with how she felt?

Why did she have to be the bigger person?

But of course, for them to entertain the thought of truly loving one another, would mean they would be risking their very lives. And Jennifer could never do that. Sebastian had been her first love.

But now she needed to believe that their love was over, and that it was time for them both to move on. By the time they pulled away, Emerick had joined them. "Your powers are truly remarkable," he said.

"That's nothing," Jennifer said. "It's just a relief being able to show people."

"Agreed," Sebastian said. "I've been battling this damn werewolf thing for six months now and today was the first time I could be honest about it. Not that I had a choice."

"Try a lifetime, Colby. Speaking of, let's head to school before we get in trouble for something else."

The car ride back to Richmont High School was silent, until Sebastian pulled up into the parking lot. "I think I might give school a miss for the day. I want to see how Daniella is doing," he said.

"Go ahead," Jennifer replied, climbing out. "Wish her the best for me."

"I will."

After they had watched Sebastian's car disappear down the road, Jennifer led Emerick towards the school's main building. It was almost half past ten and they were well and truly late for class.

While in the waiting room, they saw a bruised up blond boy sitting by the door and upon closer inspection of his almost transparent skin, it was apparent they were looking at a ghost.

"What's his soul telling you?" Jennifer asked as she and Emerick took the seats across from him.

"Somebody beat him to death, and he can't remember what they looked like."

His answer made her wonder just how many of the other ghosts around Richmont had met similar fates. Generally, spirits couldn't talk so having somebody like Emerick around sure could come in handy.

Not long after, they were joined by Principal Cindy Burrows who was standing in the open doorway to her office. The woman was roughly in her early forties, had a long brown plait down her back and was a good friend of Marian Morris and a member of her coven. While the woman wasn't actually a non-mortal witch, she did, however, possess a knack for tarot reading and a love for the musician, Stevie Nicks. "Jennifer, your mother called to tell me you'd be late. You and Emerick can both come in now."

Oblivious to the ghost boy, Cindy led Jennifer and Emerick into her office and closed the door behind them. Once they had taken their seats, Cindy addressed them. "So, late two days in a row, Jennifer. I should have you suspended. But having had your mother fill me in on all the details, I will let it slide. This time." Cindy narrowed her eyes onto Emerick. "Emerick, is it? I don't believe I have a last name for you on file."

"Gremory," he answered, low enough for them both to hear.

"Gremory?" Cindy repeated. "Why does that name sound familiar? Do you have family around these parts? Distant cousins perhaps?"

"Just my brother. He's working on a case in town."

"No parents?"

Emerick gave a half attempt at a shrug.

"They died a few years ago. It's just us and our band. I think that's why Marian invited me to stay with them. She's an old family friend."

A long bout of silence filled the air. While Jennifer had used that exact lie to fool her friends, it did make her wonder just how Emerick knew her mother. Was there a story behind their past and why hadn't Marian revealed it before?

She prayed that Emerick wasn't a long-lost brother or something. Because that would just make her attraction to him very weird.

Cindy, on the other hand seemed awkwardly enchanted by the boy, which was very out of character for the respectable principal. "Well, until we set you up with your own schedule, you can accompany Jennifer to her classes. You're both free to go."

"Thank you, ma'am," Emerick said, standing from his seat.

"Oh, call me Cindy," she gushed.

Jennifer's involuntary burst of laughter forced the principal to realize her own mistake and break free from her enchantment. "I mean, Miss Burrows. That's right. I'm the Principal. Call me Miss Burrows."

✳ ✳ ✳

"You have a real way with women," Jennifer chuckled as she and Emerick made their way through the empty corridor to their English class.

"I could say the same thing about you and your mother. That whole Morris charm is no different to my gifts."

"You keep talking about your powers, yet you refuse to tell me what you are. Can you at least tell me this? We're not siblings, are we?"

Emerick laughed. "Siblings?"

Just outside the glass door to their English room, Jennifer stopped to face him. Adamant. "Think about it. We're not that much different, you're also immune to my powers and not to mention, my mother welcomed you into our house with opened arms. I wouldn't be surprised if she did have another child out there. Promiscuity runs in the Morris blood."

Jennifer watched as Emerick considered each one of her points thoughtfully until finally he shook off the thought.

"If it puts your mind at ease, Jennifer, we're not related in any way. We're not siblings. Not cousins. In fact, the sheer prospect of us being related at all is very impossible."

"So why can't you tell me about your identity?" Again, her question gave him pause, though before he could answer, the door opened and their teacher, Mrs. Cook was standing before them. "You're both late," the short, seventy-something year old, squirrely woman said, gesturing for them to enter the classroom.

Jennifer bypassed Mrs. Cook and found her seat beside Sebastian's best friend, Marco Henderson. Marco was a mortal of African American and Puerto-Rican descent. His mother was Richmont's very own Deputy Sheriff, Olivia Henderson.

The instant Jennifer took her seat, Marco leaned in and whispered, "Where's Seb?"

Jennifer watched as Emerick chose the only empty seat left – beside Chelsea – before voicing her response to Marco. "Daniella had a headache, so they went to see my mother."

"Mama Morris to the rescue, again?"

Just as Jennifer attempted to answer, Mrs. Cook raised her copy of *The Odyssey* into the air. "We will be commencing our reading on page eighty-two, Miss Morris. I hope you have your copy. Emerick, on the other hand, will need to…"

"…He can share mine!" Chelsea chimed in, excited for the opportunity to bond with Emerick.

"Thank you, Chelsea," Mrs. Cook replied.

Chelsea's offer sent a hint of irritation to Jennifer's very depths. She knew that uncomfortable feeling well, as it was the same green-eyed jealousy she felt when seeing Daniella with Sebastian. To brush it off, Jennifer rummaged through her backpack only to find that she was missing her own textbook.

"You can share mine," Marco offered, holding up his own copy.

"Thanks."

He smiled – almost bashfully – as he shuffled closed and placed the book on her desk. Sitting so close to him, Jennifer could sense his nervousness.

While he was generally a very confident football player, he was nothing more than a mere pawn to the Morris charm. And although he had avoided asking her out in the past thanks to his loyalty to Sebastian, recently, he had been making a more obvious attempt to get to know her.

"Your perfume smells nice," he said.

"Thank you."

"Sorry if that sounded creepy, but I just wanted to let you know, I noticed."

As Jennifer's eyes followed the text of the book, she resisted the temptation to shake her head at the footballer's attempt to compliment her. If it had been any other day, she might've complimented him back and they'd be hooking up by the end of the week, but after the morning she'd been through, the last thing she needed was more drama.

As the thought of Daniella passed through her mind, she sent a mental message to her mother asking about Daniella's wellbeing. Marian's response came back almost immediately.

'The girl is fine. Sebastian is with her and they're about to call their parents to tell them the news. Sebastian will make a good father.'

As silence filled Jennifer's mind, she knew that her mother had ended their connection.

Sebastian and Daniella as parents? They weren't even out of high school yet. With only eight months left until graduation, life was already banging at their doors. Sebastian had been accepted into three of his college choices. Daniella to one.

Thanks to the lack of finance, Jennifer and Aisha were headed to community college. Chelsea's future would be wherever the wind would take her.

While her mother refused to teach her spells that predicted the future for fear of altering time and events, it didn't stop Jennifer for needing to know how everything would play out.

"Are you alright, Jennifer?" Marco asked, knocking her from her thoughts. "It's time for lunch." Brought back to reality, Jennifer looked around to see that the rest of the class, including Emerick and Chelsea, had left.

"How long have I been sitting here?" she asked, getting to her feet.

"About twenty minutes. Is everything okay?"

"I want to say yes. But the truth is, I feel like we're all about to be hit by something big."

As Jennifer tried to determine what she meant by 'big', she picked up her bag and left the classroom with Marco, right behind her.

"Like what?" He asked. "An apocalypse? I wouldn't be surprised at this school."

"No, not that big. Just… I don't know. It's just a feeling I get."

"While that sounds like the plot to a horror movie, Sebastian warned me to never doubt your instincts."

"Why would he talk about me like that?"

Marco rubbed his dark hands together, as if to prepare himself for a life changing moment. "Jennifer, I know you and I don't normally hang because of your past with Seb, but…"

"…Jennifer, you need to come. Quick!" Aisha interjected running almost right into them at full speed. She was breathless and terror was written all over her face.

"Why? What happened?" Jennifer asked.

"Emma Bryce was just found dead in the girls' bathroom!"

FIVE

A bustling crowd of students blocked the entrance of the girls' restrooms, where Principal Burrows spoke with officers from the Sheriff's department on the inside. According to commotion, they were waiting on the paramedics to arrive. Rumored whispers spread through the hallway indicating that everybody had a theory to share.

"It was a drug overdose," somebody said.

"But Emma wasn't on drugs," came another voice. "I think it was an eating disorder."

Emma Bryce was in the grade below Jennifer and while the two had never formally spoken, Jennifer could still put a face to the name.

Emma had always been one of the good students. Not one to mess up. Spotting Emerick and Chelsea, Jennifer and Aisha pushed through to crowd to speak with them. "It's so exciting!" Chelsea gushed. "Do you think we'll get news reporters?"

If looks could kill, Aisha would've committed first degree murder. "You can't be serious. A girl just died and you're thinking about how to get your five minutes of fame? Girl, don't even!"

"For your information it's fifteen minutes," Chelsea retorted.

"Yeah, but it would take a reporter just two minutes to realize that you're not worth their time, while the next three minutes would be spent with you clawing at them out of desperation as they try to remove the camera from your face, you superficial bi…"

"…Alright, enough!" Jennifer interjected. "Does anybody know how it happened?"

Aisha pulled a face, indicating that she knew more than she had previously let on.

"Do you know something?" Jennifer probed.

To Jennifer's surprise, Aisha seemed to go into a trance as she spoke in an emotionless tone.

"I was in the bathroom, and I heard… I heard people making out in the stall next to me, so I washed my hands and left. But then, a girl went into the restroom just after I did, and I heard her scream."

"The girl that went in after you. Was that Emma Bryce?" Emerick asked.

"No. It was the girl that found her body. Emma must've been…" As fear took a hold, Aisha shook herself from her trance and cried out the words in torment. "Oh my god! The killer was in there. They weren't making out he must've been..."

"Shh, Aisha," Jennifer comforted. "It's okay."

But Emerick was desperate to get more out of her. "Did you see who was in there? Did you see them leave the...?"

"...No, no, I didn't see anything. She died and I could've helped her. Oh my god! I let her die."

"No, you didn't," Jennifer said, noticing for the first time that Chelsea was no longer with them.

She scanned the crowd to see the cheerleader talking with a male paramedic.

"You need to find a way to get in there," Emerick said in a tone that only Jennifer could hear. "I don't think the killer left."

"Look after Aisha. I'll see what I can do."

Jennifer ventured through the crowd of students, trailing behind the other two paramedics as they headed into the girls' bathroom. She made it into the restrooms to find Miss Burrows and two other teachers giving their statements to Sheriff Mike, Deputy Olivia Henderson and Emerick's Private Investigator brother, Ambrose.

The paramedics circled the middle cubicle and lifted Emma Bryce's naked body onto the gurney.

Upon witnessing the sight, Jennifer's entire body froze. She could barely speak, breathe, or even hear the voices of those that surrounded her. Seeing Emma pale, motionless and drained of all life forced Jennifer to question everything she had ever believed in.

"...her out of here."

Distant voices pushed through the fog of her mind as she realized that everybody had become aware of her presence. "Jennifer," Miss Burrows said trying to shield her view of the body. "You shouldn't be in here."

"Uh..."

"Do you know what happened, Jennifer?" Ambrose asked, approaching her. "Can you help us figure out who did this?"

"She's in shock," Miss Burrows cut in. "We should be sending her to the school nurse."

"If she knows something, it might help us figure out who is responsible."

While the Principal tried to think up another reason to leave Jennifer out of the mess, Sheriff Mike approached them.

"Jennifer Morris, did you see or hear anything that might be able to help us out?"

"Yes," Jennifer stammered. "I heard what happened."

"You heard what happened?" Miss Burrows asked, her face drenched in sympathy.

While Jennifer wanted to tell them that Aisha had told her everything, the words refused to pour from her mouth.

"She's in shock," Deputy Olivia said, bringing her arm around Jennifer's shoulders. "We should take her to the station, get her checked over and have her give a statement."

"Are you sure?" Miss Burrows asked.

"Positive. Let us know if you hear anything else."

Sheriff Mike and Ambrose left the restrooms first, bracing themselves for crowd control. They were followed by the paramedics with the covered gurney. As Deputy Olivia Henderson and Miss Burrows escorted her into the hallway, Jennifer caught sight of Emerick speaking with his brother.

Judging by his disgruntled expression, Ambrose had told him to stay at the school. "Are you okay?" Emerick asked, charging towards her, only to have Olivia break in between. "She's fine, she just needs to come with us to the station."

While Jennifer wanted to tell Emerick that everything was fine, she could barely muster a word. Instead, her mind continued to plague her with the thought of Emma Bryce's corpse.

How would she ever get past seeing something like that?

✳✳✳

Jennifer was subjected to a long line questioning at the Sheriff's department. Unfortunately, she could barely articulate her thoughts thanks to the image of Emma Bryce continuing to flash through her mind. "Did you hear his voice?" Sheriff Mike asked as Olivia handed her a fresh cup of coffee.

"Are you sure it was a man?" Ambrose asked.

Jennifer knew she needed to tell them that Aisha was the one who had heard the incident occur. That Aisha should be there delivering her statement, but as she went to open her mouth, her phone rang.

"Can I... Can I answer this?" Jennifer asked, holding it up to show that it was her mother calling.

Sheriff Mike nodded. "Go on. She's probably worried about you. We'll give you some space."

Once he had led the others out of the office and closed the door Jennifer answered her phone. "Mom, it's okay. I'm…"

"…I know, dear. Emerick filled me in. Why didn't you tell them that Aisha was the one that heard what had happened? Now, if you speak up, they'll think you're a liar and we'll all be hung. Look I called to give us some time to come up with a…"

Of course, Marian would make it about her. Jennifer sighed. "Mom, relax. I'm just going to tell them that…"

"…Can you end your call for me, please Jennifer?" Ambrose's voice cut Jennifer off. She hadn't even realized he had reentered and shut the door behind him until she saw looked up. He spoke with sheer authority and while he looked to be only a few years older than her, he seemed to possess the demeanor of somebody much, much older. To Jennifer's surprise, she was unable to resist and hung up on her mother. "Thank you," Ambrose said, taking the seat across from her. "Thanks to my brother, I know you know what I'm capable of. Am I right?" She nodded involuntarily. "Good," he added. "Now, while your soul is telling me that you didn't hear firsthand what happened to Emma, it is telling me, that you know who did."

Refusing to allow herself to become a drone to a pretty face, Jennifer sealed her lips shut and broke eye contact. But again, his compulsion was far too strong. Her head stifled a nod.

What was happening to her?

Why couldn't she control herself around him?

Ambrose brought his hand to her jaw. "It's okay. I know you want to protect them. But I am not the killer. I need to stop these things from happening before this town attracts the attention of the hunters. Do you understand me, Jennifer?"

His fingers brushed along the surface of her skin, mesmerizing her in a way she couldn't shake.

His crystal blue eyes made her feel as if she was drowning. She needed to swim to make it to safety. But she was losing her battle for self-control. "You're a very strong witch, Jennifer. Your powers, your gifts... they're remarkable. But you don't need to use them against me. Let me in. Tell me what I need to know, and we can protect those girls together."

He was merely inches away from her face and there was an unrelenting force pulling her towards him. She wanted to kiss him. To taste his lips. To tell him everything he needed to know and more.

She wanted Ambrose. Needed him even.

In her mind it was as if she could hear him singing only to her and as powerless as she felt to resist, her Morris charm reveled in the man's attention. A fool to her own desire, Jennifer met his lips with hers and before she could come to her senses, he kissed her right back. The moment their lips met Jennifer felt a powerfully ecstatic wave rush over her followed by an incredible weakness.

A vulnerability that brought with it, visions of darkness and screams of terror. But then, amongst that darkness, she saw two blue eyes peering out at her, telling her that he would protect her. Before she could determine just who she was looking at, their union was broken by Ambrose pulling away.

"Don't worry, we'll get to the bottom of this," he said, as if nothing had just happened.

"What the hell was that?"

"What was what?"

"I'm not stupid. What did you do to me?"

Ambrose flicked through his notes than looked back up at her. "Your soul just told me that you're off the hook. You can go now."

"But you kissed me!"

With an irritating twist of events, Ambrose raised an eyebrow looking seemingly confused by the very notion of having done such an insane act. "Did I?"

✳✳✳

By the time Olivia escorted Jennifer to the parking lot, Marian had been waiting in her brown range rover, worried sick. Noticing Jennifer's shaken state, she hurried out of the car to assist her into the seat. As Jennifer buckled her seatbelt alongside her mother, her eyes drifted to the time on the car's stereo. It was 3:52pm.

How was that possible?

For that to have been the case, would've meant that she had spent two whole hours kissing

Ambrose, which he denies happened in the first place. "Hey mom? Is that the right time?"

"Of course, it is."

Jennifer nodded, but her confusion only escalated. Nothing of her situation made any sense.

While pulling onto the road, Marian's eyes landed on Jennifer. "Cindy told me what you saw today. It's understandable just how terrified you might be feeling. I have some tea for…"

"I don't want tea. Is Emerick home?"

"He is. But Sebastian and Daniella left an hour ago." That was good news. She needed to speak with Emerick. Alone. She needed answers.

Ambrose had clearly done something to her head. Had he spiked her coffee without her realizing? She needed to be assured that Ambrose wasn't the killer and only Emerick could give her the answers she sought.

Once Marian pulled into their driveway, Jennifer didn't even wait for the engine to stop before she raced into the house, up the stairs and into Emerick's room without even knocking to see if he was in. "What the hell are you?!" she demanded, taking in the sight that he wasn't even wearing a shirt before he could react. If she hadn't been attracted to him before, the sight of his muscular body dressed in only a towel and the shimmery blue amulet which hung from his neck, as he faced her would've certainly changed that concept entirely. Evident by the surprised look on his face, mixed with his wet hair, and the water droplets to his skin, he had only just hopped out of the shower.

"Jennifer? Are you okay? What happened?"

"What do you think happened? Your brother kissed me, and half a day disappeared from my life."

"He... kissed you?" Fear, or maybe anger flashed across his face.

"Yes. To make it worse, I wanted him to. I don't even know him. Eww! I feel so dirty."

Before Emerick could react, Marian burst into the room in a fit of her own fury. "I told you, Emerick, that if either of you hurt my daughter that there would be consequences. You promised me!"

"You knew what they were?" Jennifer snapped at her mother. "Why didn't you tell me?"

"Of course, I knew. I just didn't think they would be so stupid to try anything on my own child. But what can you expect from a demon?"

The word *'demon'* rattled Jennifer's very core. Demons were the lowest, most powerful forms of non-mortals that existed. And furthermore, they were very rare to come across. Gutted, she turned to Emerick just in time to see the remorse in his eyes. "I'm sorry. I didn't mean for that to happen, Marian. I'll pack my things. Thank you for your hospitality, I won't take up any more of your time."

He turned towards his bed, collecting an assortment of clothes, and giving Jennifer a full view of his back, which was riddled with long scars as if he had endured a lifetime of lashings at the hand of another. "Mom?" Jennifer stammered, gesturing to his back.

"Yes, Jennifer. He's a demon from hell. Scars come with the territory. Now come on, let's leave him to get dressed." As Marian held open the door for her to follow, Jennifer resisted.

"No, he's not leaving. Emerick didn't do anything wrong. His brother did."

"They're incubi, Jennifer. And now his brother has the taste for your soul. Don't think he'll stop there. They're like ravenous vampires. Only worse. They don't need an invitation to enter our house. After one kiss, Jennifer you can become his mindless slave. The next kiss could kill you."

Marian's anger turned from Jennifer and back to Emerick who was now standing beside them. "You promised me..."

"Yes, I promised," Emerick spoke up. "And I upheld that promise. But Ambrose..."

"Emerick tried to come with me to the Sheriff's office," Jennifer cut in. "But Ambrose stopped him. You always told me to go with my gut and right now my gut is telling me to trust Emerick. Maybe he can teach me how to resist Ambrose's compulsion. Or maybe there's a spell to make me stronger."

By then, all attention was on Jennifer and the room was in an uncomfortable state of silence, until Marian finally broke it again.

"Emerick, do you believe there's a way for Jennifer to resist the compulsion of your brother?"

"I haven't heard of one yet, but I'm willing to help her find one. And if we don't, you have my word that when we find out who is responsible for the deaths on those mortals, I will take Ambrose as far from here as possible."

"Good. We'll leave you to get dressed. Come, Jennifer." This time as Marian left, Jennifer followed her close behind. When they got to the stairs, Jennifer asked her mother, "You don't think Ambrose committed those murders, do you?"

"No, I don't. This killer has a different face. But I do feel that Ambrose and Emerick are our only way of stopping whoever it is, just, please, promise me that you'll be careful."

As Jennifer promised her mother that she would be as careful as she could be, she couldn't help the niggling feeling she received in the pit of her stomach. Until then, the only boy she had ever felt powerless to resist had been Sebastian. She had been head-over-heels in love with him since before she had even known what love was.

But now there was another person in her future that she would grow to love more than time itself.

That very being was the same person whose blue eyes she had seen in the darkness. She just couldn't work out whom those eyes belonged to.

SIX

Over the next few weeks, Emerick and Jennifer worked together extensively in search of not only who the killer might be, but also if there was a spell to make Jennifer immune to the incubus curse.

And as they worked, Jennifer couldn't help but feel the insatiable pull that Emerick seemed to have over her.

One Saturday afternoon, when the two were sitting in Marian's summoning room poring over the Morris spell book, with Marian working at her cauldron, Jennifer considered an alternative approach to finding answers for the incubi protection spell. "What if we just asked Ambrose?"

Of course, Marian was quick to argue. "You will do nothing of the sort. He might be acting as a Private Investigator, but he is the last person in the world that I would trust around you. Wouldn't you agree, Emerick?"

"Your mom's right. You don't need Ambrose thirsting for you. He'll turn you into a groupie."

"A groupie?" Jennifer chuckled. "Your band is good, but I'm not going to follow you on the road."

"That's just what Ambrose calls those he kisses and keeps alive. Our drummer, Katie and our keyboardist, Dan, are amongst them."

It was an interesting concept. Marian had already said that Jennifer was at risk of being one for having kissed Ambrose once. But Jennifer didn't feel any different. She just felt it might prove a useful alternative to the answers that Emerick didn't have. She was just about to voice that opinion when Marian chimed in, holding a small silver flask.

"Jennifer, I need you to take this ambrosia tea to Daniella. She is currently over at the Colby estate and I'm not in the mood to speak with that wretched old Fernando, today."

Fernando was Sebastian's father and while he and Marian certainly had a past, it was one the woman refused to speak of. In fact, whatever had happened between had caused a serious rift between them both. Which meant that Jennifer and Sebastian always acted as the messengers between households. "Are you ever in the mood to speak with him?" Jennifer asked, rhetorically.

"Don't get that tone with me, go... The pair of you!" Marian held the flask out to Jennifer, which the girl took before leaving the summoning room with Emerick. As they walked the twenty-minute distance to the extravagant Colby estate, Emerick couldn't help but ask, "Are you sure you're alright seeing him with Daniella?"

"I don't see what you're getting at. Sebastian and I are fine."

"You're a fool if you believe that. Every time the two of you are together your souls tell an entirely different story."

Jennifer stopped in her tracks, utterly stunned. She had never thought about what her soul might've been doing when she was around Sebastian. But here was the chance to dive into that curiosity. She turned to Emerick, looking him squarely in the eyes. "And what exactly are our souls saying?"

"It's not exactly what they're saying. More like what they're doing."

"Okay, so what are they doing?"

Emerick froze. It wasn't like him to be caught off guard. He looked away in a bid to gather his thoughts then explained in a way that could be easily spelled out.

"Jennifer, when the two of you are together, your souls are quite literally... Well, they're..."

It was then that she understood. And it came to her as sheer surprise that he had even brought it up at all. The very prospect that hers and Sebastian's souls were *'going at it'* when they were simply talking was... Hell, it was awkward, that's what.

Jennifer couldn't help but laugh it off. "Oh, my goddess. Emerick, that was... that was good. You made a joke. I get it. It's funny because of the whole incubus seeing souls and the whole sex thing... It's really funny."

"I'm not joking. That's actually what happens. When the two of you are together."

The moment couldn't get more awkward if they tried. Jennifer considered the warm flask of tea in her hands and the fact that they were halfway to the Colby Estate.

"Thanks for that explanation, Emerick. Here, you deliver the tea." She tried to hand over the flask, but he wouldn't take it.

"I can't. Sebastian doesn't like me. I think he can smell what I am. You need to do it."

Defeated, Jennifer continued walking with her focus on her feet. "I really wish you hadn't told me that."

"Sorry. But you asked, and I didn't want to lie."

With than newfound knowledge, Jennifer approached the door to the elegant, white building and was about to leave when it was opened before her by Sebastian, who was standing in the doorway with an optimistic look on his face.

"Jennifer? I thought I sensed you."

Jennifer sent an awkward glance to Emerick before handing the flask to Sebastian. "Here, my mom asked me to give this to Daniella. Sorry, but I can't stay. Emerick and I need to..."

"...No don't go," Sebastian replied, taking the flask. "You should come in. My mom made those cookies you love. You could at least make her happy and help us eat them." That was a cheeky move on his behalf, but sadly, it worked.

Jennifer smiled. "You're a horrible friend, Colby. I haven't had them in... what's it been...?"

"Three years."

"Right, three years."

Jennifer and Emerick followed Sebastian into the luxurious living room, where they found Daniella sitting on the white colored couch. On the elegant glass coffee table sat a large plate filled with homemade chocolate chip cookies. Anamaria's own secret recipe. On seeing Jennifer, Daniella stood to greet her, just as Sebastian handed her the flask of tea. "Jennifer's mom sent her over to give you this," he said.

"How did you know I was here?" Daniella asked as Jennifer and Emerick sat on the couch opposite her. "Ah..." Jennifer began. But before she could improvise, Sebastian took the lead.

"I messaged Marian and told her you were here. I didn't want you to suffer another traumatic incident like you did in the car." That was a clear lie, but Jennifer welcomed it entirely. The last thing she needed was Daniella finding out the truth about her identity. As Sebastian sat beside Daniella, Jennifer's mind went right back to what Emerick had said about their souls. And as her eyes rested on Sebastian who had the hint of a smile at just seeing her, she couldn't help but feel highly uncomfortable. She reached for a cookie and focused all her attention on not choking on the delicious snack. "Wow, this is awkward," Daniella said, noting the silence.

"What's awkward?" Jennifer and Sebastian asked in unison. Emerick broke into an involuntary laugh and Daniella turned to Sebastian. "Is everything alright between you two?"

Taking her cue to leave, Jennifer stood and headed for the door with Emerick right behind her, but Sebastian rushed after them.

"No, don't leave. I need to speak with you," he told her.

"I'm sorry, I have to. Emerick and I have other plans." Sebastian turned to Emerick, in concern, then back to Jennifer before speaking in a quieter tone. "You do realize what he is, don't you?"

"Of course, and it doesn't change anything. I still need to go." As Jennifer and Emerick headed outside, Sebastian rushed out after them.

"Please, Jennifer. Just let me speak to you in private, okay?"

Putting aside how awkward Emerick's explanation of their souls made her feel, Jennifer reluctantly agreed to speak with him a few feet away from Emerick right beside a red rose bush.

"I can't believe you're hanging with a demon. I didn't realize it at first, but..."

"...Just tell me what it is that you need to tell me." Jennifer replied.

"Oh, right. It's just... I was chatting to my dad, and he told me that you and I should have a telepathic link thanks to the curse. Apparently, he and your mom have one, too."

"A telepathic link? Are you sure?"

"It's like that thing you share with your mom, only it's with me. That's how dad told your mom to bring the tea. I was wondering if you wanted to give it a try. With me."

While the thought made her wonder just what Emerick would see with their souls this time,

Jennifer was curious to see if the whole telepathic link thing, did work.

"Alright. Let's try it. Can you hear my thoughts?"

She mentally sent a telepathic message voicing her skepticism. *'I really doubt this is going to work because you're not a Morris Witch. You're just an obnoxious quarterback.'*

He grinned, proudly. *'Ha. It worked. Obnoxious, huh? Can you hear me?'*

'Sure can. Wow, this is so cool. And such a change from my mother's voice in my head all the damn time. Are you able to do it with your dad?'

'No. I think the connection has to be made by you. Just a heads up, stay out of my head ninety-nine percent of the time. You don't want to see what goes on in here. It might disturb you.'

Jennifer burst into laughter as his confidence came through within his thoughts.

At least through their telepathic communication, she could fill him in on the whole awkward soul truth that Emerick had imparted on her earlier.

'Did you want to hear something weird?' she asked.

'Can't be as weird as this is. But sure.'

'Well, Emerick is an incubus. He can read souls and you won't believe what he told me about our souls.'

Sebastian's surprise about Emerick being an incubus brought sheer concern to his eyes. So much so, he spoke out loud.

"Wait, an incubus? Jennifer, you need to be very careful around him. Just don't sleep with him, alright?"

"Shh..." she said and gestured to her head. 'Don't worry about that. But do you want to know what he said?'

Sebastian sent a warning look to Emerick, before turning back to Jennifer. *'What's that?'*

'So, don't be weirded out by this, but… Apparently, whenever you and I are together… he thinks our souls are… hooking up.'

The humor in Sebastian's face was unmistakable. He grinned. She thought he'd burst into laughter, but instead, he only thought back to her.

'Well, I'm not surprised. Sex is on my mind ninety-nine percent of the time, and something tells me that you think of it fairly often too.'

Jennifer froze. Bit down on her lip. How the hell did he know that? And how dare he voice it when Daniella was inside his house?

'What makes you say that?' she asked, praying it was just a guess. But he merely smiled a knowing look. *'We're connected. I can sense your feelings.'*

'Really?'

Sebastian nodded. *'Yep. When you're mad, scared, happy... horny."*

Humiliation took over Jennifer's entire body. "What did you just say?!"

He tapped his head and continued speaking telepathically.

'Naww. Don't be embarrassed. I can't help it. I feel it all... Including those nights when you're tucked up in your bed and feeling...'

He was disturbing. Beyond disturbing.

"Has anybody ever told you how disturbing you are?" she snapped out loud.

Sebastian merely shrugged. Proud of the thought.

"Oh goddess, I feel so bad for Daniella. How she has the patience to deal with you is beyond me. I need to go!" Jennifer closed the telepathic link and stormed over to Emerick.

"See you soon, Morris." Sebastian called out as he headed back inside.

But Jennifer didn't look back. Instead, she snapped at Emerick. "You and Sebastian are very horrible people."

"Why? What did I do?"

"You told me about our souls. How bad was it this time?"

Emerick grinned. "You really don't want to know the answer to that."

✳ ✳ ✳

Instead of heading home, Jennifer's frustration over Emerick's ability to read her soul took her to the Sheriff's department to speak with Ambrose. Knowing that Jennifer would go with or without his help, Emerick accompanied her to ensure that Ambrose didn't take advantage of her.

Unsurprisingly, their conversation with the posing Private Investigator drifted to the murder case. "There's been another murder," Ambrose said. His concern, evident.

"Any suspects?" Emerick asked.

Ambrose shook his head. "Not yet. Aisha gave her statement, but there was nothing of use. Tried to ask for my number too."

"Leave her alone!" Jennifer scolded.

"Relax, she was never in any danger of me... I've always preferred the challenge."

His overly charming smile made Jennifer feel slightly uncomfortable, as if she was a mouse in a lion's den. But then he continued.

"Anyway, this new murder happened last night at Richmont Park."

"Richmont Park?" Jennifer asked. "But that's so close to my house. You don't think they're onto Emerick, do you?"

"Why do you think I'm so concerned about it? Whoever it is seems to be much stronger than either of us." As Ambrose stared at Jennifer with that almost hypnotic look, she wondered if she would be strong enough to take him on with her powers. But the more she peered into his eyes, that very curiosity was replaced by a sense of false admiration. Infatuation. Lust.

"Stop it, Ambrose!" Emerick snapped, forcing Ambrose to remove his hold on her. Jennifer blinked out of her trance, while Emerick continued. "Yes, she's a Morris witch. But that doesn't mean you need to add her to your personal collection of groupies."

"Don't tell me you haven't thought of what she might taste like. Her lips are like nothing I've ever tasted before. Hint of lavender mixed with something far more intoxicating. But then again, you're probably out of practice. How long's it been? Three hundred years?"

Had it really been three hundred years since Emerick had last kissed somebody?

"I said stop it," Emerick snarled.

On that second warning, Ambrose relaxed his demeanor.

"Alright, you're safe for now. But I'm not sure how long that will last. That Morris charm really is alluring."

"That's actually why we're here," Emerick replied. "We need a spell that will keep her immune from our compulsion."

"I've never heard of such a thing."

"You haven't?" Jennifer asked, getting back to the matter at hand. "There has to be something. Do you remember anything about when you were first made into what you are? Was it a witch that did it or something else?"

As Jennifer asked her questions, Ambrose focused his attention entirely on her. He seemed amused by her need for answers and Jennifer couldn't tell if he had the answers she sought or if he was just being a patronizing ass.

"Are you really going to ignore me?" she asked, turning to Emerick who had a far off look in his eye.

"Don't take my silence as an insult, Jennifer," Ambrose said. "It's almost impossible to answer any of those questions ourselves. It's been a very, very long time. There is only one being who does have the answers and unfortunately, there is no way of contacting her."

"Her?"

"Her name is Gremory," Emerick said.

"Gremory? But that was the name you gave Miss Burrows."

"Yes, it was. And Gremory is in hell. Well, at least she should be."

"Why? Who was she?" Jennifer asked.

"A dangerous demon."

"She wasn't just any demon," Ambrose added. "She was a duchess of hell. Beautiful. Powerful. And one hell of a queen in the sack. She led twenty-six powerful demon armies and for those who had the pleasure of meeting her... Well, let's just say that meeting her was like being in the presence of a god."

"I take it you two were close?" Jennifer asked Ambrose.

"Intimately. But, as Emerick said, she's in hell."

"And that's where she can stay for all I care," Emerick replied.

"To Emerick, Gremory is somewhat of a sore subject," Ambrose mused. "She possessed him in a way that made him swear off mortal souls forever. Sad story. Me, on the other hand, I'd do anything to pull her in close, run my hands up those thighs, and well... I guess this isn't exactly the conversation to be had in front of young ears such as yours,

Jennifer." Jennifer glared at him, but he merely smiled in delight. The guy was utterly useless at offering up any useful information.

But maybe there would be a way to communicate with Gremory. Maybe trap her in a demon trap and torture her for information. Just maybe...

"I know what you're thinking, Jennifer, and the answer is no," Emerick said, interrupting Jennifer's thoughts. For a moment, Jennifer had forgotten he could read her soul. Just as Ambrose could too. Still, she needed to persist.

"But if Gremory can help us we need to try."

Ambrose laughed. "She really is cute, isn't she? Now, I see why you prefer to stay at Morris Manor. Maybe she should take a job here as my receptionist. It would really boost my..."

"No!" Emerick and Jennifer said in unison.

"We're done here, anyway," Jennifer added, getting to her feet.

"About time," Emerick replied, following her.

As they reached the door, Ambrose called after them. "Good luck. Just let me know if you hear anything on that killer."

His statement reminded Jennifer of the very crippling notion that not only was the killer still out there, but they had also struck again.

And this time, so very close to her home.

SEVEN

At the small table in Marian's summoning room Jennifer and Emerick worked with the old spell book and crystal ball. Both of which had been in the Morris family for centuries.

Marian had allowed them the use of the space to work on a protection spell for Jennifer before she had gone on her date with the Sheriff. She had also emphasized the point that Emerick would find himself the target of a vicious revenge spell if he even thought of making a move on her daughter.

Jennifer waved her hand over the crystal ball.

"I need you to focus. Try to think back to when this curse was first placed on you, can you remember a face or anything that can help me conjure up an image?"

She studied the expression on his face as he tried to focus. It was almost adorable. After a moment, Emerick shook his head. "It was just so long ago. Thousands upon thousands of years ago, I believe."

"Are you really that old?"

"Yes. Hence my frustration at paranormal romance novels. Why any being whose been around for that long would choose to stalk a teenaged girl is beyond me."

"Yet, there you are all brooding and mysterious and you don't even look a day older than eighteen."

"I'll take that as a compliment. Now, where were we?" Jennifer rubbed her temples with her knuckles at a loss for ideas, until the glimmery blue amulet that hung from his neck stole her attention. She loved how it looked as if there was a violent storm tucked inside.

"That amulet... What's with it?"

In a poor attempt to hide it away, Emerick closed his fist around the swirling blue, before reluctantly, slipping it from his neck to show her. "This is what stops me from devouring the souls of mortals."

Upon closer inspection of the light blue stone, Jennifer found herself mesmerized by the white, dark blue and black particles that flashed through it recklessly.

In fact, the very color of the pendent could only be compared to the blue in Emerick's eyes.

"Can I touch it?" she asked.

"Yes. But be careful. That very stone contains millions of souls all taken from some of the vilest demons in hell."

As Jennifer held the cold trinket in her hands, his words chilled her very core.

"Actual demons from hell? How does it work?"

"When I feel the need to devour a soul, I clasp the amulet in my hand and focus. It satisfies my hunger. But only for a short period of time. Unfortunately, I still can't be intimate with another person."

"Does Ambrose have one?"

Jennifer handed back the necklace and shivered at the thought of unleashing those souls onto the earth. "He does, but he still loves to play dangerously. He also has a better hold on his abilities than I'm willing to risk. He loves the power he holds over people almost as much as Gremory did." As Emerick thumbed the silver chain in his hand an idea formed on his face.

"What if you use this as an anchor? It's the most important possession I've owned since I became what I am."

"It's worth a shot. Close your eyes." Jennifer placed her right hand over his, encasing the amulet between them, and waved her left hand over the crystal ball with full focus.

"Show me the past. Show me what I seek. Show me the answer to my own protection."

As quickly as she spoke the words, a sudden force emerged from inside the amulet and radiated up her arm like a violent burst of energy. Her eyes slammed shut and her entire body convulsed.

As if something had a hold of her, Jennifer's chair flung backwards sending her crashing to the floor. "Jennifer!" Emerick cried. Her body thrusted about, violently, as if she were at the very thrall of an epileptic fit. When it was all over, her eyes fluttered open to see Emerick crouching over her. His eyes gaped in sympathy and regret.

"I shouldn't have let you do that. Are you alright?"

But Jennifer felt fine. Or at least she thought she did. "I think I did it," she said, retaking her seat.

Jennifer waved her hand over the crystal ball, focusing on her intent and waiting for the ball to deliver her answers. Within seconds a blur of red and black smoke filled the ball. And amongst the smoke, images started to take shape. But they changed so fast, she could barely keep up. Nor could she understand what they meant.

She could've sworn she saw Emerick in what she believed to be hell. Just as she saw herself and her long line of Morris witches dating throughout time.

To get a better understanding, she waved her hand in a swirling motion and asked, "Am I powerful enough to withstand Ambrose?"

Again, the red and black smoke changed shape. This time it resembled the word, *'Yes.'*

That was a good sign. But Jennifer's intuition told her to ask the question that was truly on her mind. So, silently, she mouthed the words.

To that question, the answer she received frightened her. A highly complicated message written in the form of eight distinct words, *'Prepare for a battle of head and heart.'*

As Jennifer tried to understand the meaning behind the words, Emerick reminded her of his presence. "What did it tell you?"

"It told me that... Well, whatever just happened, the ball believes I'm strong enough to deal with Ambrose."

Jennifer got to her feet and would've fallen over, were it not for Emerick's fast reflexes.

"Are you alright?" he asked.

"I'm good. I think that spell just tired me out a little. Why don't we go watch TV instead?"

With a subtle nod, Emerick escorted her downstairs and into the living room.

While Emerick went through the large collection of movies, Jennifer couldn't help but feel far weaker than she had all day.

If she could be entirely honest, she would say that something had gone drastically wrong with the spell. But what that error was, she wasn't sure.

Halfway through their science-fiction movie, Emerick turned to her, looking very confused.

"You look like me in algebra, Emerick. What's wrong?" Jennifer asked.

"I can't read your soul. That's never happened before."

"What?"

Emerick positioned himself closer to Jennifer on the couch, studying her as if trying to read her thoughts. "Normally, your soul won't stop talking. But now... I don't know."

"My soul doesn't stop talking? You can't be serious!"

A cocky smile spread across his face. "It's not as bad as Chelsea's... But it's like you have this desire to impress the world with who you are. Brave, capable, confident. Now, that light is gone."

"That couldn't sound creepier if you tried."

"Sorry, but maybe the spell did work. Maybe you are immune to my kind."

That assumption was news to Jennifer's ears. "How would we know for sure?"

"You would need to test the theory by kissing one. If they cannot consume your soul, that's how you know. But in this case, I'm not willing to test it out."

"Why not? Aren't I the kissable sort?"

Emerick's body stiffened. "You know that's not the case."

"But if it's to test out the spell, technically, it would be better to do it now, than when we actually need to work."

Adamantly against the idea, Emerick got to his feet. "No, Jennifer. I'm sorry, but even for that reason, I'm not willing to risk it. The last thing I want to do is hurt you."

Jennifer grinned, deviously. "So, you're not the least bit curious as to whether you *can* kiss me? Or even what it would be like to... you know, have..."

"...Oh, I'm very curious. But we shouldn't even be talking about this. The killer was at the park last night. And while Aisha heard that girl making out with somebody, she didn't remember seeing anybody leave the bathroom after her. That..."

Frustrated, Jennifer studied him. She really wanted to kiss him and not just to find out whether the spell had worked, but because she would've had to have been blind not to. His piercing blue eyes seemed to stare right through her.

The overconfident smile that crossed his lips brought about thoughts in her that she needed to tame. He was an incubus who hadn't even kissed another girl in goddess knew how long. That very thought was not only poetic but made her curious to test out those boundaries just for the sheer sake of doing so. Natural seduction. Danger. And Jennifer wanted every inch of him.

Noticing that she was still staring, Emerick addressed the subject that was obsessing her mind.

"I don't need to read your soul to know what you're thinking. Can we please just focus on the matter at hand?"

"Alright, fine. Sit down. If it helps, there are vents in the girls' bathroom."

Intrigued by that news, Emerick sat beside her. "Vents? Were they opened? Closed? Can you remember?"

"I didn't get a good look. There were so many people, and the paramedics were..."

As the thought of Emma Bryce's deceased body flashed through her mind, Jennifer struggled to string along her sentence properly. "...They were... Well, they were putting Emma's body on that bed. Her clothes had been removed... discarded as if whoever did it didn't care about her at all. Why would anybody do that?"

"Sounds like all the other girls. Whoever is doing it can disappear so easily without anybody seeing. We need to check out those vents. Maybe..."

While Jennifer watched Emerick's lips move as he explained the plan, she couldn't help but think about how short life was. Emma had died so young. Had Ambrose not pulled away that time during their interrogation, Jennifer might've died too.

Yet, Emerick had lived for centuries and even forgotten the last kiss he had shared with another.

Jennifer didn't think. Instead, she cupped his chin in her hands, brought her lips to his and kissed him, passionately. The moment she did, she was hit by an immeasurable surge of power rushing from her lips and igniting every inch of her body.

It made her feel more powerful, more alive than she had ever felt before. While Emerick's first reaction was to linger for a moment, he quickly came to his senses and pulled away. "What the hell, Jennifer? I could've killed you!" Again, he got to his feet. Not regretting her action for a minute, Jennifer stood to oppose him, relishing the warm tingling sensation prickling through her. "Yeah, but you didn't. In fact, you've no idea how rejuvenated that kiss made me feel."

"What?"

Jennifer smiled. The radiant energy coursing through her veins could push her to run a marathon, if she chose.

"That spell and all the events of today had me exhausted, but kissing you... I don't know. It made me feel so much better."

Silence filled the room as Jennifer studied the confusion on his face until he finally spoke up again.

"Maybe that spell forced me to share some of my essence with you in a way that built an immunity."

"Like a vaccination or something?"

Judging by the shrug of his shoulder he was just as in the dark as she was. "I guess that's possible," she said.

Emerick inched closer, studying her as if to be looking for a subtle change in her demeanor.

He brought his hand to her face and stroked her jawline.

"What are you doing?" she asked.

"As I said before, I can't see or even read your soul. It's like... like we're equal."

"Oh thanks. Yes, because I'm *just* a witch, while you're an all-powerful..."

"...Not what I meant. Besides, the Morris witches are very well-respected, even in the demon..."

Keeping up her overly confident façade, Jennifer refused to let him keep talking.

She pulled his head to hers and kissed him again. This time with more intensity than the last.

Emerick's hesitation lasted no longer than a few seconds before he wrapped his arms around her and returned the kiss as if the very fate of his existence depended on it.

✳ ✳ ✳

Almost fifteen minutes had flown by as Jennifer and Emerick rested on the couch lost in one very passionate kissing session. As Emerick's lips traced her jawline, Jennifer wondered just how far they could take things without either of them devouring the soul of the other.

"Is this where I admit, how irresistible I've found you from that first moment in the club?" Emerick asked, bringing his kiss to her ear.

"So, Ambrose was right. I do have an effect on you."

"In more ways than one. I sensed you in the audience that day at the concert and your soul lit up like an angel. It was the brightest thing I've ever seen. Hence why I had to buy you a drink and keep you away from my brother."

"An angel? Do they really exist?"

Emerick pulled away to brush her nose with his.

"Of course, they do. Many demons are either fallen angels, corrupted non-mortals or even cursed mortals. Angels are a rarer breed than we, but they can be just as merciless when provoked."

Jennifer thought for a moment. His information made her question something of her own lineage.

"Do you think that's just the Morris Charm? That bright light you saw?"

"No. Not at all. Your mother has no charm on my kind. Nor has any other Morris witch I've met in the past. It's just you. You're an anomaly and it's been driving me wild not to be able to touch you like this..." As he spoke, he ran his hand up her arm, to her shoulder and then to her neck. His eyes glazed over as he watched her. A thousand thoughts ran through her mind, but at the very top of that list was Emerick.

She wanted him more than she ever thought possible, and it was a shock to the system because she barely knew him. She had felt that pull back at the concert. That enticing, dangerous power he had over her. But he held back out of fear of what he could do. Jennifer pushed a lock of his hair out of his face then kissed him again.

She had the power to turn a dangerous demon into a lovesick puppy and it fulfilled her more than she could fathom. She wondered how many other Morris witches had possessed such power in the past. Before she could lose herself again, she heard a patrol car pull up outside and knew that her mother and Sheriff Mike had just arrived from their date. "Mom's back!" Jennifer announced, breaking their connection.

Without giving Emerick a chance to react, she chanted, "*Teleportatio*," then disappeared from the couch, and reappeared in her bedroom, dressed in her pajamas. From downstairs, Jennifer could vaguely hear Emerick greeting Marian, so she quickly crawled into bed and feigned sleeping just in time for her mother to open opened her door to check on her. "Do you really think I'd fool for that, Jennifer? Please, I invented feign sleeping."

Jennifer sat up in her bed. Busted. "Hi mom. How was your date?"

Marian groaned. "Oh, goddess. I just hope the two of you worked out a protection spell."

"I think we did. Can I ask you something?"

"You can ask me anything, dear," Marian said, taking a seat beside her.

"Have you ever met an angel?"

Jennifer watched as Marian froze at the very mention of the word 'angel'. After a long bout of silence, Marian prepared herself to answer Jennifer's question. "I should've seen this coming inviting a demon to stay."

"I'm sorry?"

"Jennifer, your father was an angel. He was sexy, and so self-righteous. But the moment he laid eyes on me... Well, all that self-righteousness went right out the window. Now, didn't it?"

Jennifer fell into disgust as her mother went into vivid detail. "He didn't look like all those priests believe. Oh no, he was just a stranger at a bar. Blond hair, blue eyes, faded jeans. I knew he wasn't a mortal or a non-mortal from that moment. And when he followed me to my motel room, we…"

"…Okay, mom! Enough. Alright! Gross. I don't need to know the details. But how did you know he was angel?"

"How didn't I? When an angel is willing to make a connection with you, you bear witness to a bright, almost blinding light. Not to mention, they make the most incredible lovers."

Getting to her feet, Jennifer raised up her hand to silence her mother. "I'm never sleeping or eating again. Oh, my goddess, that was so gross."

"Sorry. But why do you ask? Did Emerick say something?"

Jennifer thought back to how he had seen her light from the club. And about how he believed it had disappeared.

"Do I have a light?" Jennifer asked.

"I've never seen one in you. I'm not sure. Maybe it's because you're my daughter? Or maybe it's clouded because you're a Morris witch? If you like I can do a little research."

"That's okay, mom. That won't be necessary."

"Okay. Only if, you're sure."

Marian went to leave the room until Jennifer called out behind her. "You never said how your date with the Sheriff went."

"I thought you didn't want to hear me kiss and tell."

"No, you're probably right. Goodnight, mom."

"Goodnight, Jennifer."

Without another word, Marian flicked off the light with the wave of her hand, and left, closing the door to Jennifer's bedroom.

But as Jennifer turned onto her back, she pulled out her phone to text Emerick. *'You're an amazing kisser. I'd love to do it again sometime. I also want to know more about this angel light thing.'*

Emerick's quick reply brought an excited smile to Jennifer's face. *'I'd love to do it again too. We'll look into it together. Goodnight.'*

'Goodnight. X.'

Without another word, Jennifer placed her phone on the cabinet beside her bed and rolled over to go to sleep.

EIGHT

Jennifer awoke feeling far more exhausted than she normally did on a Monday morning and it wasn't due to a lack of sleep.

While she and Emerick had been pulling in overtime for research, they had also been testing out the incubi immunity as often as they could. Which meant frequent secretive make-out sessions whenever they got the chance.

As Jennifer entered her room from her adjoining shower, draped only in a towel, she was startled by a knock on her bedroom door.

With her intuition telling her exactly who it was, she opened the door with a sultry smile planted firmly on her face. "I'm surprised you're still knocking," she said to Emerick.

"What can I say? I'm a gentleman," Emerick grinned.

"A gentle demon more like it."

She pulled him into her room, forcing him into a passionate embrace as she closed the door behind them. The more they kissed, the more her exhaustion dissipated and the livelier she felt.

"Mmm. You're better than coffee," she said, breaking the connection.

His hands rested at her hips and for the first time he noticed that she was in nothing more than a towel. His eyes glazed over. They hadn't gone that far yet, but the yearning was certainly there.

Their lips lingered merely inches apart, both thinking the exact same thing. But before either could give in to their desires, Marian's voice called out from downstairs.

"Jennifer, I hope you're dressed! Breakfast is at the table."

"We should stop before we get too carried away," Emerick said.

His words were filled with a sheer burning desire, which merely indicated his repressed urges, but they both knew he was right.

Emerick kissed her mouth one more time then fled the room, shutting the door behind him.

Smiling, Jennifer pressed her back against the door, feeling ready and rejuvenated to start the day.

She flicked her wrist and in an instant her damp hair was now dry and styled perfectly. Her towel turned into a blue shirt and a pair of black pants. And for that exact reason, she couldn't have loved magic any more than she did.

In English class, Jennifer took her seat between Sebastian and Marco. She was surprised to see

Sebastian back at school as his on-campus presence had been very unpredictable since finding out he was expecting a child.

Daniella, on the other hand, had taken to home schooling out of fear of what the other students might think of her predicament.

As usual, Emerick took his seat, unwillingly beside Chelsea. Fortunately, Jennifer had remembered her copy of *The Odyssey* and would not need to share with Marco again.

"If you ask me, '*Romeo and Juliet*' is a much better story," Marco said, drawing the attention of Jennifer and Sebastian.

"You think so?" Jennifer asked.

"Of course. Warring families, forbidden romance where the lovers would rather die than be apart? What's better than that? If I was a teacher, that's what I'd teach."

Jennifer and Sebastian exchanged looks, but it was Sebastian who voiced his opinion. "I see your point, Marco. But let me top that with *Beauty and the Beast*. Strong, wonderous woman tames a ferocious beast."

"Dude, the beast locks her up! Strips her of everything. She has no choice but to fall victim to him. They have a word for that and that's…"

"…You guys sound like girls," Jennifer laughed, utterly amused by their conversation. Fortunately, it wasn't loud enough to draw the attention of Mrs. Cook who was thoroughly immersed in her own book.

"Well?" Sebastian mused. "As the official girl here, care to weigh in?"

"You want my opinion?" she asked them both.

"You've never steered me wrong before, Morris."

Marco nodded in agreement.

"Alright," Jennifer began. "But for the record, you're both right. While I would rather see Juliet pick up a sword and protect herself, the whole forbidden romance thing is pretty hot. I don't know any girl who doesn't love a good love triangle. And in relation to *Beauty and the Beast*? While the Beast looks like a monster, he's really just a cute little puppy with a bark worse than his bite. It'd be like rescuing an abused dog whose so scared at first, but then you teach him table manners and how to do his business outside the house. Besides, that whole monster in the sack thing... Well... Makes a girl wonder."

While her answer forced Sebastian to bite his fist to hold back a barrel of laughter thanks to their inside joke, it merely brought out an intrigued smile from Marco. "You're interesting, Jennifer. You don't meet too many girls like you."

"Thank you, Marco." While Jennifer got back to reading, she picked up on the vibe Marco was putting off and so did Sebastian. Marco was clearly biding his time to tell her how he felt. As she caught a glimpse of Sebastian glaring at his friend, Jennifer knew she needed to step in.

She opened the mental connection with Sebastian as her eyes focused on her book. '*Let it go, Sebastian. He's your friend. Besides, I'm not into him, like that.*'

Sebastian furrowed his brow. '*You're not? Okay good. What about the new guy? I get that he's staying with you but...*'

'*Seriously, Colby? You get no say on who I'm with. You're with Daniella, remember?*'

She looked at him and Sebastian's thoughts came to an abrupt halt. His eyes flashed amber and he turned away, indicating that she had struck a nerve.

But honestly, Jennifer didn't care. She turned to Emerick who couldn't look more bored if he tried.

Of course, he would've been bored. He was probably around when *The Odyssey* was first written. Jennifer glanced down at the words in front of her and was hit by a sudden pang of dizziness. But as soon as the dizzy spell hit, a vision passed through her mind.

It was accompanied by an intense headache. The more images that flashed through her mental vision, the fainter the pain to her head became, and the easier Jennifer found herself slipping into the fantasy in her mind.

She was in a luxurious bedroom, surrounded by mahogany furniture and red and gold linen.

The stench of smoke engulfed her senses. But she wasn't afraid or in any danger. Nor was she alone. She was dressed in a beautiful, green gown with a tight bust and a puffy underlay. The very scene made her feel important... Almost, godlike.

Foreign lips pressed against her back. Another set kissed her wrist. She was being worshiped by two guys. Though, who they were, was a mystery.

The man at her wrist brought his kiss to her lips and his face became visible. It was Emerick.

She pulled him just as his lips parted. Instead of kissing him, she devoured a white transparent essence which poured from his mouth like frost in the cold. *His soul.*

Hungrily, Jennifer inhaled his spirit as if her life depended on it. And when there was nothing left of it, his lifeless body dropped from the bed to the floor. *Dead.* But Jennifer wasn't finished her feast. She turned her head to the second stranger, only to find herself mesmerized by the brown and amber eyes peering back at her. Sebastian.

His very scent, intoxicating and musky. Like walking through a forest in the springtime.

Jennifer kissed him with an overwhelming passion. And as his soul poured from his mouth and into hers, he began to transform.

Jennifer inhaled the last of his spirit and watched the black wolf take over his entire body. Owning it.

Sated, Jennifer patted the fierce wolf as if it were nothing more than her pet.

'Damn Morris, and I thought I had warped sex dreams.'

Brought back to reality, Jennifer was horrified to find that Sebastian had just seen her vision.

Of course, she had forgotten to close their mental link from earlier and to her surprise, they were still sitting in English class.

"Sebastian," she whispered. "That wasn't a sex dream. That was a vision."

"A vision? How do you know?"

"Trust me on this. I do. And whatever it means, it can't be good."

✳ ✳ ✳

After class, Jennifer stayed back to talk to Emerick and Sebastian about the vision. Not that she needed to explain too much to Sebastian as he had witnessed the entire thing. As Emerick paced the room trying to determine what the vision meant. "Do you normally get visions like that?" he asked.

"Visions, yes. I just haven't had one in a while. And while normally they hurt really bad but that one..."

"You totally looked like you were enjoying it," Sebastian smirked from the desk beside her. "But then, I don't blame you. It was pretty hot. Especially that part where we..."

Jennifer buried her face in her arms. "...I really wish I'd ended that damn mental link. Why did you have to see that?"

"Actually, it's rare moments like this that make me love the Morris-Colby curse."

On Sebastian's words, Emerick came to his own conclusion. "That has to be what it is. Perhaps the curse has an impact on the incubi immunity. Maybe that's why you saw us both in the vision."

"Wait," Sebastian looked directly to Jennifer. "You're immune to incubi? How do you know?"

"Emerick and I did a spell so his brother wouldn't be able to compel me."

"How does it work? Have you even tried...?"

Jennifer held Sebastian's gaze long enough for him to get the point. They were supposed to be talking about her vision. "Alright, point taken. At least you left Lobo alive. In the fantasy, I mean."

"Lobo?"

"That's his name. It's tradition that we name our wolves after our first transformation. And if it's any consolation, I think he likes you."

"Well, that's obvious," Emerick cut in.

"What's that supposed to mean?" Sebastian asked.

"Jennifer's soul is one of the few souls Lobo appears loyal to. Even your friend Marco doesn't make the cut."

"Why do you think that is?"

"I'm guessing he sees himself as Jennifer's familiar. Could help explain the curse."

His words shattered through Jennifer's entire understanding of the Morris-Colby curse.

She had heard that witches often owned familiars. Yet, she was deathly allergic to cats and seemed to possess some sort of natural affinity to ward off all other animals. She couldn't even keep a goldfish alive.

Judging by the contemplation on Sebastian's face, Emerick's words had left him in his own trail of thoughts. "How does Lobo feel about Daniella?" Sebastian asked.

"Why don't we go back to the problem at hand, instead?" Emerick asked, rubbing the amulet at his neck. "I think Jennifer's vision might have something to do with Gremory."

While he had made the gesture subtly, Jennifer had not only seen it, but was also tempted to ask for a dose of soul inhalation.

"Gremory?" Jennifer asked. "Do you think she might be calling out to us from hell?"

"If that's the case, we need to be very careful. If we can find out whose killing those girls, maybe then we can work out where those visions are coming from and what they mean."

"Sounds like a plan," Jennifer said, getting to her feet. "Sebastian, don't you have training?"

"I do. But I just wanted to make sure you were okay," he said, making his way towards the door.

"Well, I'm fine. So, go. You don't want to be late." On her say so, Sebastian took off out the door, with Jennifer and Emerick slowly following behind.

While Sebastian disappeared down the corridor, he sent an over the shoulder wave to Aisha who rushed towards Jennifer.

At the very sight of Aisha, Jennifer's excitement escalated. They ran into each other's arms and squealed. "Oh, my goddess, Aisha! It feels like forever since I've seen you."

"I know right. My mom has me seeing my therapist again," Aisha said with a tone that would win her an academy award. "It's so bad. She and dad are walking around on eggshells in front of me. I can't stand it. But hey, at least Joey's back from college. Huh?"

"Aisha, you've been traumatized. Of course, they would be worried about you. How is your brother anyway?"

"He's good. He's been seeing this one girl for almost a year now and..."

While Jennifer was sincerely curious to hear about Aisha's overachieving brother who had always been the apple of the girl's eye, she was interrupted by her mother telepathically using her as a messenger again. "Dammit!" Jennifer said, pulling away.

"Excuse me?!"

"No, I didn't mean you, Aisha. I just forgot I need to tell Sebastian something. Can the two of you wait, right here?" she asked looking to both Aisha and Emerick. "I promise I'll be right back."

"Sure," Aisha said.

Jennifer took off down the corridor and caught up to Sebastian just as he exited the building. "Sebastian, wait..." she said, puffed out.

"What's up?" he asked, stopping immediately and smirking at the way she struggled to catch her breath.

Jennifer tried to relay the words that her mother had said. But her breath had escaped her. "My mom... my mom wants me to tell you..."

"Damn Morris, pace yourself. You didn't run that hard."

No, she hadn't run that hard. Her exhaustion had just hit her harder thanks to having undertaken the slightest cardio. That wasn't normal. It must've been the damn incubi immunity thing.

"Come with me," Sebastian said, pulling her to a nearby tree to sit on a wooden bench. "Sit down and take a breath."

Jennifer did. But as her breath returned, she was met by the sheer exhaustion that took over and the incredibly overwhelming temptation of Sebastian's lips, as he sat beside her.

"So, what did you need to tell me?" he asked.

"Wow, that was crazy. Anyway, my mom just told me to tell you that... Damn, your lips look amazing."

"Ah... what?"

Upon realizing what she had just said, Jennifer could've passed out... And not just thanks to the exhaustive side effect of the incubi immunity.

"I'm sorry, that wasn't what I was meant to say."

"It wasn't?"

Another exhaustive spell took a hold of her, and again she was looking at his lips. But she wouldn't kiss him. He was dating Daniella and she was with Emerick. Sure, they weren't public about it, but they were still a 'thing'.

If she had had the energy, she would've run right back to Emerick and kissed him for that simple rejuvenation she needed, but she didn't.

Instead, she was forced to relay the message that Marian refused to tell Sebastian's father herself. "Forget what I just said back there."

"Forget it?" he mused. "But you just said my lips look..."

"...Shh. My mom said to tell your dad that there was a wolf attack just outside of town." That had Sebastian's attention, so she continued to speak through her fatigue. "Mom was called into help with... to help the victim but..."

"But what...?"

Jennifer couldn't take her fatigue any longer. She needed his lips. Needed his energy. So, against her own willpower, she kissed him. And what was worse, was that he kissed her back with that same urgency.

It was almost as if fireworks had gone off all around them. The kiss was sizzling, magnetic, and unbelievably hot.

But above all else, Jennifer's energy levels returned. Her thoughts went to the vision of her devouring Sebastian's soul. The very thought terrified her.

She ripped herself away ready to face the lashings of having done the worst thing imaginable in the history of their friendship.

"Oh, goddess. I really shouldn't have done that! You're with Daniella, I'm... Well..."

Sebastian ran his tongue along his bottom lip, with a delightful smile. Clearly enjoying the situation far more than she was. "That's okay. We'll just blame it on the incubus thing, okay? It's totally fine."

"It is?" But she knew it wasn't.

Thanks to her own selfish needs she had just kissed the father of her friend's unborn child.

And while in so many ways that was a sin, the worst sin of all was that she had loved every minute of it. She needed to bury those emotions and get back on with her message as if nothing had happened. "As I was saying. There was a wolf attack just outside town. My mother covered for your father. She even compelled Sheriff Mike to not look into your..."

This time it was Sebastian who didn't let her finish. He kissed her, as if he had been waiting to do so forever. And thanks to the damn Morris-Colby curse and Jennifer's inability to resist, she kissed him right back.

✲ ✲ ✲

It had been ten minutes since Emerick had rubbed the amulet to satisfy his soul craving as he,

Jennifer and Sebastian ran through the possible theories behind Jennifer's vision.

But since those few minutes he was beginning to get that feeling again. It was as if he was struggling to maintain a hold on his own sense of reality.

He was standing with Aisha waiting for Jennifer to return. While he had lost track of where she had gone and why, she had promised that she wouldn't be long. But in that moment, he needed her to hurry.

"How has your brother been?" Aisha asked him.

"He's been... he's been good," Emerick replied.

But then, something clicked in him. It was as if a switch had just been flicked inside his mind. And suddenly, he wasn't Emerick anymore.

NINE

Days passed and while Jennifer and Emerick actively poured their time into solving the murders. Secretly, it was Jennifer's way of keeping her mind distracted from the kiss she had shared with Sebastian.

That kiss had left her highly rejuvenated and surprised that she hadn't consumed his soul in the process. However, it had left Sebastian in such a state of stunned silence that he had taken more days off school. Jennifer found it frustrating that Aisha was also absent.

Apparently, the day that she had returned, she had come to tell Jennifer she was leaving town to spend some time with her older brother.

Unfortunately, Aisha had left before Jennifer had returned from her encounter with Sebastian and so she had received the information secondhand from Emerick.

The current day was Thursday. Jennifer and Emerick were sitting at a bench under a shady tree, poring over a notepad scrawled with theories pertaining to who the killer might be.

To their disappointment, that was the one day that Chelsea didn't have cheer practice.

While Emerick and Jennifer hadn't yet gone public about their relationship, Emerick was still in the uncomfortable situation of warding off Chelsea's constant passes.

Either she didn't seem to register his message, or maybe she did, and just loved the chase.

"I still think it's Ambrose," Jennifer said.

"Just because you don't like him, doesn't mean he's a murderer," Emerick replied.

"I hear he's holding a party," Chelsea chimed in, barely listening to their conversation. "We should go, Emmie bear."

Jennifer choked on her own laughter. "Emmie bear?"

Emerick stared at Chelsea as if the girl was nuts. "You really need to understand, Chelsea. It's just not going to happen between us."

Without waiting to hear the rest of the conversation, Jennifer got to her feet.

"Well, I'm heading to the bathrooms to check the vents. If Ambrose is the killer, then I'm suspecting he doesn't want us to check there."

"Wait, Jenny," Chelsea said, getting to her own feet. "I'm going to the bathroom too. Let's go together."

"Wait, what?" Jennifer stammered, looking from Emerick then back to Chelsea.

"You know, girl talk. Besides, if there is a killer around. We'll be safer together, right?"

Before Jennifer could even think of arguing, Chelsea looped her arm through hers and led her away from Emerick, towards the bathrooms.

❋ ❋ ❋

As Chelsea spoke from inside the closed cubicle, Jennifer muttered along barely listening to the girl's infatuated bragging of Emerick.

She stood at the sink, examining the vent which hung open in the upper right corner of the wall. There also seemed to be a dark smudge pressed against it. A handprint, maybe?

"So, do you think I should ask him?" Chelsea's voice sounded out as she opened the door to the cubicle and approached Jennifer at the sink.

"Ask who?" Jennifer startled.

"Weren't you listening? I want to ask Emerick to the party tomorrow night. I think he's really into me."

Jennifer couldn't help the light smirk that crossed into her cheek at Chelsea's request. Chelsea going to the party with Emerick was a bad idea.

The guy was an incubus who could only kiss Jennifer. She had no doubt he would only turn Chelsea down. "How do you know he likes you?" Jennifer asked, with a tone that made her sound like she cared.

"How else? The guy listens. I could tell him anything and unlike the guys on the football team, I feel like he won't judge me. Besides, don't you think he'd make good arm candy?"

Jennifer was in total agreement. Emerick did make good arm candy. With Chelsea waiting for an answer, Jennifer shrugged. "Yes, he does. But please don't get your hopes up if he says no. He and I..."

Jennifer had no idea where her sentence was going. She stopped.

"What are you getting at, Jenny? Are the two of you together?"

Jennifer considered the question. Were they a couple? If they weren't then what was stopping Emerick from saying 'yes' to Chelsea?

Oh, right! The curse. But Chelsea could be very cunning when she wanted to be. Stuck on the spot, Jennifer fessed up. "Okay, here's the truth, Emerick and I... Well, we've been hooking up."

Jennifer felt her entire body swoon as she pictured his lips against hers, until she was pulled back into the moment by Chelsea's hard to read stare. "You and Emerick?"

Chelsea shrugged off the thought. "That's fine. May the best girl win."

"Wait, what?"

Chelsea charged out the bathroom headed for who Jennifer could only imagine was Emerick. But before Jennifer could follow, she was brought to the floor by another overwhelming wave of exhaustion.

On her knees and drained of all energy, Jennifer tried to send a mind message to her mother. But it was as if her powers were temporarily unavailable.

"Oh, goddess!" Jennifer stammered trying to pull herself to her feet. It was a struggle. Almost as if she had a ton of weight resting on her shoulders.

She reached for her phone, only to find that it wasn't in her pocket. She must've left it on the table.

Jennifer looked up to see a girl standing by the wall watching her and wearing what would've only been in fashion a hundred years ago. Clearly, she was a ghost. But Jennifer didn't care.

"Please, you need to help me," she groaned. "Find Emerick. Please!"

But the ghost shook her head and disappeared into the wall behind her. Jennifer had no choice but to find him herself. She would not die on the bathroom floor and count herself as another of Richmont High's ghosts.

With all the strength she could muster, which wasn't much at all, Jennifer clambered to crawl out the door, leading into the corridor.

It was still packed with students. She called out to whoever might hear her. Her breathing was rough. Rapid. Her exhaustion felt as if she was on the cusp of death.

"Jennifer!"

A familiar voice called back to her. But she couldn't look up to see who it was. As two strong arms dressed in the blue and white football uniform, wrapped themselves around her, she knew she was in the arms of one of the footballers.

"Sebastian?" she pleaded.

"No, it's Marco. I'll take you to the nurse."

Jennifer stared up at him as he carried her through the hallway. Sweet Marco. A mortal, but strong enough to hold his own. Her eyes rested on his dark lips. Mesmerized.

The physical exhaustion of her own body was crushing her very soul. Something told her that kissing Marco would make it all better. And for that reason, she needed him. "Marco," she stammered.

But he spoke with authority to the nurse. "We need to do something. I found her like this."

"Bring her to the bed." Nurse Violet, a mortal woman with dark hair and dark eyes, in her forties told him.

With Jennifer ready to pass out in his arms, Marco placed her on the bed as Violet tried to assess the girl. "Jennifer, did you take something?"

Jennifer tried to shake her head, but her eyes went back to Marco's lips. Her focus drowned out all noise as he spoke to the nurse on her behalf.

At some point, Violet rushed away to get something, leading Marco to turn his gaze onto Jennifer.

"It's okay, she's going to get..." Before he could finish his sentence, Jennifer launched her lips onto his and kissed him. Hungrily, he kissed her back and as Jennifer's strength returned, she felt the strength in him diminish. His hold on her weakened and soon, Marco collapsed on the bed beside her, unconscious.

"Oh my god!" Violet gasped in horror, dropping her tray of medicines to the floor. The only advantage to the hell that Jennifer was in was that her energy levels had returned back to normal.

TEN

Horrified by the sight of Marco's unconscious body, Jennifer jumped to her feet. "It's okay, I can fix it!" she stammered. While she wasn't entirely sure if she could, she knew she had no choice but to try.

"What did you do to him? Is this some kind of spell?" Nurse Violet barked as she made her way to the bed.

"In a matter of thinking..." Jennifer stammered. "Wait, how do you know about...?"

"Do you think I'm stupid, Jennifer? I'm the school nurse and non-mortals aren't as big a secret as they like to think. But what did you do? This doesn't look normal."

Nurse Violet checked Marco's pulse, then sighed a sense of relief. "Oh good. He's only unconscious. Now, tell me what you did so I can fix it!"

On the woman's request Jennifer struggled to determine where to begin. Should she tell her about Emerick? "Come on, Jennifer! What did you do?"

"Ah... it's a... it's a love spell!"

Well, it was kind of a love spell. Just not the typical sort of love spell one might make. Still, Jennifer continued with her lie. "I wanted to make him like me back."

Nurse Violet tsked as she adjusted Marco on the bed, making him more comfortable.

"This is why witches need to learn the value of manipulating the wills of others. Hold his hand. You're going to need to channel some of your energy into him. You'll also need to cast a Forget spell."

"Make him forget?" Jennifer asked.

"Yes, Jennifer. Do you really want to traumatize him? Or even worse, have a lovesick footballer on your hands? Those spells never turn out well. Well? What are you waiting for?"

Despite the nurse's clear experience dealing with non-mortal incidents, Jennifer wondered if her idea might actually work. Fortunately, sharing energy spells were the simplest to cast.

She closed her eyes and covered Marco's hand with hers, praying with every ounce of her magic that it would work. It wasn't until Nurse Violet sighed in relief, and Marco spoke up that Jennifer opened her eyes. "Wow, Jennifer. That was one hell of a kiss."

After a look from Nurse Violet, telling her to deliver the spell, Jennifer touched her hand to Marco's forehead. "Forget the kiss," she said. "Forget everything that happened in the past ten minutes."

Jennifer removed her hand, allowing him to sit. "What's going on?" he asked. "What am I doing here?" Jennifer looked to Violet, waiting for the woman to fill him in.

"You suffered a concussion on the field and Jennifer was nice enough to bring you to me," Violet said. Clearly a rehearsed line. "You can go now, Jennifer. But you, Marco, will need to stay for further observation."

On her command, Jennifer left leaving Marco in the bed. This was one matter that she needed to divulge to Emerick. And fast.

✳ ✳ ✳

When Jennifer found Emerick, he was at his locker gathering his books for the next class. "Can we talk?" she asked. Without giving him the chance to respond, she pulled him into the nearby cleaning closet and flicked on the light.

"I was hoping for a bit of privacy," Emerick said, cupping her face and leaning in. But despite her own temptation, Jennifer held up her hand in front of his face. "This is urgent, Emerick. That spell... I think... I think it made me an incubus."

A slight smile radiated into his left cheek.

"The female word is succubus and why do you think that?"

"Because..."

Jennifer hesitated to tell him. And not only because the truth was hard to explain, but because tears had welled up in her eyes at the very thought of what she had done to Marco. Still, Jennifer told him. And not just about the kiss with Marco, but also about her kiss with Sebastian.

"I thought I could handle it... But it's like... Well, it's like something is taking over my body. I feel so weak at first, but then... I just feel so much better afterwards. Oh goddess, Marco almost died because of me."

A flush of emotions, ending in relief flashed across his face. "He's okay, though?"

"Yes. I performed a sharing energy spell on him... Then a Forget spell. Emerick, I..."

As Jennifer tried to pour out her heart, Emerick brushed his nose against hers, sweeping her into a wave of silence.

"Think about it. You didn't hurt Sebastian, remember? Clearly, while you may pose a light danger to mortals, you've only been affected a little bit. I promise you, Jennifer. Everything will be fine. Okay?"

Accepting his promise, Jennifer kissed him, relishing the very embrace that only his body could give.

He lifted her up, her legs wrapped around him and as his lips found her jawline, she knew they needed to stop before they got too carried away.

"We should... We should stop," she puffed. Emerick's eyes glazed over as he pulled away.

But he obeyed. Reluctantly.

"You're right. Not here. But I have a question."

Jennifer adjusted her clothes and her sanity as she looked up at him. "A question?"

"Come to that party with me tomorrow night? It's actually at Barrett Manor. Ambrose suggested we play an alcohol-free gig for those who want to see us perform but aren't allowed to drink."

"The party? You do know that Chelsea was going to ask you, right?"

The flash of a smile crossed through his eyes.

"She did but I turned her down."

"What about your brother? Are you sure we can trust him?"

"Sheriff Mike will be there to ensure nobody gets out of hand. Hence, the no alcohol rule."

"No alcohol? Really? And who would want to go to an event that's being supervised by..."

But Emerick's pleading eyes won her over. "...Alright, I'll go. Just so I can watch you perform. But Barrett Manor? Really? Not even my mom will step foot in there."

Emerick kissed her, overly excited for a demon. "Great, it means a lot that my girlfriend will be there watching me on stage."

"Let me get this straight. You're a centuries old demon with a love curse and you've just labelled a high school girl your girlfriend? That's so sad!"

"So true. But you're not just any high school girl. You're a Morris witch. Powerful, seductress, you could very well be a demon."

Jennifer rolled her eyes, but her stare did not waver until Emerick gave a non-committal nod and said,

"Okay, yes. It couldn't get more tragic romance novel if we tried."

"You're so tragic." Giggling, Jennifer pushed him up against the closed door, stood on her tiptoes and gave him a light, chaste kiss before pulling away again. "But yes, I'll go with you."

While Emerick closed his eyes, waiting for her to kiss him again, Jennifer opened the door from behind him, and left.

As Jennifer strode through the corridor, she couldn't explain the insurmountable power that surged through her veins.

Might it have been the energy she had consumed from both Marco and Emerick mixed in with the Morris charm, but every eye was on her.

She felt beautiful, irresistible, dangerous, and judging by the attention that was on her, she was powerful. It was no wonder Ambrose loved what he was.

❋ ❋ ❋

As Jennifer picked her seat in math class, she was surprised to see Marco return with all the confidence and enthusiasm the school knew him for. As he high fived his friends and looked her way with a large smile, Jennifer saw it. The adoration he had felt for her before the kiss had been magnified, somehow. Marco looked to the blond stoner sitting in the seat beside Jennifer with an intense stare. "Out of my seat," he said, knowing damn well it wasn't his seat.

"Dude, this is my seat. Back off, man."

But Marco swept the guy's books off the table in one swift motion. "I won't say it again. Move."

Marco wasn't normally the type to play the jerk, but something had changed.

Jennifer glanced over at Emerick, sitting two seats in front. He pulled out his phone and got to texting just as Jennifer's attention was diverted back to Marco who had just succeeded in taking the seat beside her.

"Hey," Marco said. "That kiss was pretty amazing. I would've preferred if you hadn't left me at the mercy of Violet, though."

Jennifer could've sworn she had made him forget. "What are you talking about?" she asked, just as she felt the buzz of her phone in her pocket.

Marco brought her knuckles to his lips and with an eerie look in his eyes, he whispered, "Violet thought she could stop our love, but I stopped her."

"Wait. What did you do?"

Marco shook his head. "Nothing. It's not important."

As Jennifer tried to determine what his eerie words meant, she read the text message from Emerick.

'You turned him into a groupie.'

✳ ✳ ✳

"I thought only true incubi could make groupies," Jennifer said to Emerick, after class.

"I guess not."

"Well, we need to reverse it. We need to do something to stop..." As she spoke, she gestured her head to Marco just as he approached, giving Emerick an icy stare. "...That."

Eager to get away, Jennifer stormed towards the exits.

"Where are you going?" Emerick asked as he and Marco followed her. Jennifer turned to them and clicked to the fact that Marco was prepared to follow her anywhere.

"I'm heading home. And you, Marco, you need to go home too. Forget me. Do that, please."

She willed with every level of magic that it would work.

"I can't go home, my love. I have training."

Jennifer cringed at the word, *love,* but at least his football training would be the perfect distraction. "Okay, good. Go to training. Do whatever. Please, just..."

"Can I kiss you?" he asked, hopeful.

"No, just... Just go to training."

As Marco left, Jennifer turned her anger back onto Emerick. "We're fixing this. We're seeing your brother. Now!"

✳ ✳ ✳

"You should've kissed him," Ambrose told Jennifer after she and Emerick had sought him out in his office and filled him in on their predicament.

"Maybe coming here was a mistake," Jennifer said.

"I'd love to agree," Emerick began. "But Ambrose has had more experience with devouring the souls of mortals than anybody I know."

"And I'm willing to do whatever it takes to master my own abilities. Unlike my brother," Ambrose chimed in. "Alas, you came to the right person. Now that Jennifer is one of us, she needs to..."

"...She's not exactly one of us," Emerick interrupted. "It was just a spell to keep her safe from you. To build an immunity to your charm."

"*My* charm? She's the one with that Morris lure."

"Alright," Jennifer cut in. "We need to think clearly. How do I balance out these damn urges for souls and free Marco from...?"

"The only way to stop groupies from being groupies is to find something to distract them,"

Ambrose replied. "Or by having a stronger incubus compel them otherwise."

"Another incubus?" Jennifer asked. "Well, that's sorted. You guys can do it."

"I would," Emerick began. "But it's complicated. I..."

"What my goodie-two-shoes brother is trying to say is that he has no real experience dealing with groupies and I... I just don't want to. I have more important things to deal with... Like a murder case, for instance."

"Here's hoping that football works," Jennifer grumbled. But Ambrose missed the irritation of her tone.

"Only if he really loves it. And even then, it's only temporarily. But when his coach says training is over, expect to see him waiting at your house. And unfortunately, groupies struggle to learn the word 'no'. Which really does have its perks. I mean you can get a top up of their tasty souls whenever you need it... Not to mention, the sex... If you can prolong that thirst..."

The far-off smile that fell across Ambrose's face was enough to make Jennifer cringe. "You're disgusting!"

"The alternative to making groupies is having them die in the soul devouring process. That's so much worse than lovesick lapdogs."

As Jennifer shook off the many thoughts that his words imposed, Emerick tried to consider what his brother had just said. "Prolong the thirst? Why have I never heard of that?"

Ambrose shrugged. "Because you've never tried it. You've chosen to abstain from sex. But to answer your question, 'prolonging the thirst' as I like to call it, is where we devour the soul slowly. Building up the tease, so to speak. If you're hooking up with two lovers at the same time, you only devour a piece of each soul. Neither will die... Unless you're very, very hungry."

Jennifer blushed at the thought of hooking up with two guys at once, as it brought back the vision that she had experienced in English class.

She caught the highly annoyed look of Emerick, and did her best to conceal her embarrassment, while Ambrose continued. "The way to stop ourselves from consuming a soul is to let ourselves feel what the other is feeling as we kiss them. Feel their weakness. The moment we feel their weakness, we stop. Immediately. Then do something else, stop kissing their mouth or even pull out."

"That's enough," Emerick said, noticing the chuckle that Jennifer couldn't help but release.

Ambrose was a sex addict and it mirrored something inside her that she preferred to keep buried deep down... As Marian would've called it, the Morris charm.

Ambrose loved who he was and did what he could to not harm others. In fact, he had just removed himself from her murder suspect list for that very reason and had added himself to her list of interesting people.

She brought her gaze to Emerick, who continued to glare at his brother. "Ambrose, thank you for reminding me of why I chose to stay with Jennifer and Marian. You do realize that you're giving my girlfriend sex tips."

At the word, *'girlfriend'* Ambrose picked an emotionless tone. "Surely, you jest."

But Emerick's expression indicated that he wasn't joking. "How could you be so stupid, Emerick? She's a teenaged girl. There is no 'forever'. You know that. And what's more, is that she's a Morris witch."

"What's wrong with me being a Morris witch?" Jennifer broke in, not expecting the way Ambrose took her hands in his.

"Don't tell me your mommy never told you what happens to anybody who falls in love with a Morris witch, sweetie."

"I know about that. But Emerick's a demon. He's not a mortal or even a non-mortal. I doubt that…"

"…That doesn't matter. Your father was an angel, right? Where is he now?"

Jennifer considered his question. She had no clue where her father was, nor *who* he was. Before either she or Emerick could argue, Ambrose continued. "My point is, you're both cursed. Jennifer's young, beautiful, and a powerful non-mortal. Don't cage her up, brother. Or it won't turn out well for either of you."

They took in his words. Was he right? Sure, it made sense. But Jennifer couldn't help but feel that overwhelming pull, every time she stared into Emerick's blue eyes.

They were the same in some ways. Unable to give their hearts entirely thanks to the curses that plagued them.

In that moment, Jennifer's mind went to Sebastian. Why it did, she wasn't sure. She felt that maybe it had something to do with their mental link. Was he hurting? Frightened?

Expecting to see a message from him, she checked her phone. There was none.

Breaking the silence, Emerick got to his feet. "Thank you, Ambrose for being entirely useless, yet again."

"Anytime brother," Ambrose smiled as Jennifer put her phone away and got to her feet. "Just remember what I said, Jennifer. Having groupies isn't so bad when you get used to it. Now, I have a murder investigation to get to the bottom of, so if you could close the door on the way out, that would be greatly appreciated."

He waved them out, and as they left it was almost as if an entire weight had been dropped on them.

One that made Jennifer feel as if she was headed for a very destructive turn of events.

✳ ✳ ✳

"That's why I refuse to listen to him," Emerick said when he and Jennifer were seated in her living room, later that afternoon. Her mother had gone out to her coven's weekly poker game, leaving Jennifer and Emerick home alone.

"He was just being realistic," Jennifer replied.

"Realistic wouldn't have been telling you to use the boys at your school as groupies. Have you any idea how dangerous that is?"

"Of course, I do. But I was referring to the whole you and me thing. It's going to be difficult at best.

The odds are quite literally stacked against us. So maybe we should…"

"…End things before they've barely begun?"

"I was going to say see where we go, but if you're…" Before Jennifer could finish her sentence Emerick kissed her. And it was hot.

Almost as if the very thought of not being allowed to be together in itself was its own form of aphrodisiac.

Jennifer welcomed his kiss as her tongue danced with his and her back pressed into the couch. His lips trailed to her chin, to her neck and then to the neckline of her shirt daring to go further. But then he stopped. "Do you want me to keep going?" he asked.

She knew by the look in his eyes what he was referring to. Of course, she wanted him to but before she could voice her response her phone rang from the coffee table.

And thanks to that damn mental link they shared, she didn't need to read the caller ID to know who that Sebastian needed to speak with her.

ELEVEN

Jennifer rushed the twenty-minute walk to the luxurious Colby Estate in merely half the time it would have normally taken.

When Sebastian had called to speak with her, nothing would've stood in her way. Not even Emerick who was currently waiting for her at home. She found the handsome quarterback on the old garden swing outside, where they had spent so much of their youth staring up at the stars.

His dark eyes were bloodshot from tears and vacant. Clearly, the feeling she had received in Ambrose's office earlier had been linked to whatever had broken his heart.

Sebastian's blank stare only altered when he noticed her standing before him.

"What's the matter?" She asked. Remaining silent, he got to his feet and invited her to follow him to the beautiful fountain, by the large garden shed. When they were in what must've been the nicest part of the Colby Estate, Sebastian peered down at her in the same way that he had always done when they had been together. As if she was the only girl in the world and he wasn't worthy to stand before her.

He took a breath and finally spoke. "Daniella and I broke up."

"You...?" she stammered. "I'm so sorry, Sebastian. This is because I..."

"No. It's not your fault. It was a mutual thing."

"What about the baby?"

"We're going to co-parent. Our parents know. Daniella..."

As Sebastian struggled to find the right words, Jennifer tried to make sense of their reality. Why were those words music to her ears? They shouldn't have been.

Still, she listened as Sebastian opened up to her. "Daniella can't even look at me knowing what I am. She said that I scare her... and that... She said that our baby is a monster."

The words were crippling to Jennifer just as they were to Sebastian. Calling a non-mortal baby, a monster was unbearable. But it was the lived-in reality for what they were.

If Daniella understood what Jennifer truly was, not just a girl with a mother who specialized in herbal remedies, she would call her the same thing.

It was no wonder Sebastian related to the story of *Beauty and the Beast* on a personal level. Though, he was anything but a monster.

He was sweet, caring, and smart, and any child he would produce would be the same.

Jennifer brought her thumb to the tear running down his right cheek. "You're not a monster, Sebastian."

He held her hand in his and stared deep into her eyes. The familiarity of the look between them screaming out in silence the unspoken truth. That the two were made for one another.

"There's more to it, Jennifer," he added.

"More? More to your break-up?"

"Our kiss that day... The one we had at school. I can't stop thinking about it. That's what love should feel like... Not what I have with Daniella. You and I should be together. We love each other and I know you feel it too, because I can feel what you feel."

Jennifer felt as if her world had come crashing down. How dare he say that to her when she had been trying to move on?

She stood frozen in her tracks, praying that the ground would swallow her whole. "Say something," Sebastian said. "Just say it out loud that you feel what I feel. That you think of me just as much as I think of you. We were destined to be together. I know it. You know it. Hell, even our parents know it."

Jennifer looked past him at the beautiful garden she was in. She wanted to look at anything but his face. She couldn't have him know that she loved him so much more than she should. For if they were to throw caution to the wind, the curse would ensure his life would be cut short.

When Jennifer remained silent, Sebastian caressed her face. She stared into those eyes that had driven her wild her whole life. Those eyes that still drove her wild. She forced herself out of her trance.

"We can't do this, Sebastian," she stammered. But that was a lie. A lie to keep herself safe from the inevitable pain that they could go through.

But in that moment, she truly didn't want to be safe. So, she forgot about Emerick, about Daniella and Sebastian's unborn child.

She forgot about the curse that trailed all the men that had ever loved a Morris woman. And she forgot about the soul sucking curse that she was currently battling with. All she saw was Sebastian.

"Why not? I know you feel it too. Just say it. Just tell me you love me," he pleaded.

She couldn't say anything. Instead, she kissed him. And he kissed her back.

Locked in their embrace, Jennifer remembered Ambrose's words. To feel what the other person was feeling. She focused on Sebastian.

On his need for her. His hunger. His love and his thirst for her. She was his weakness the one person who could truly tame the beast inside of him.

But as quickly as she let herself feel it, she pulled her lips away to catch her breath. His soul was much stronger than Marco's had been. Much more resilient.

But before she could pause to prolong her need for him, he kissed her again, bringing his hands to the skin of her back. The very thought of him sent her urges into overdrive. She was losing her own self-control and she was desperate to pull away.

"Sebastian," she said breathless. She hated herself for doing it. His eyes opened.

"What's wrong? Was it something I did?"

Jennifer bit down into her bottom lip, subconsciously trying to stop herself from saying the words she was about to say. "We can't do this.

You need to get back together with Daniella. You're having a kid together."

"But I want to be with you," he argued. "If this has something to do with the curse just know that I'd rather risk my life just to be with you, than go with out you. I love you, Jennifer."

She could've slapped herself. Instead, she clenched her fists down by her sides, praying for the strength to do what she needed to do.

"I know that. I do. And you know damn well how I feel about you."

"No, I don't. Why don't you tell me?"

"Seriously, Sebastian. We can't do this. Daniella's pregnant and you being with her is the right thing to do. You know that, and so do I."

Sebastian silently considered her words. Or maybe he was looking for a way to win the argument. Whatever the case might've been, he finally conceded.

"That damn Morris curse," he snarled. "I need you to go. Now!"

"Dammit! Don't be so..."

"I mean it, Jennifer!" for the first time ever, he raised his voice at her. "Get lost! Go!"

Not wanting to argue further, nor let him see the heartbreak on her face, Jennifer turned on her heels ready to leave. But before she could disappear from his sight, she added.

"Don't worry, Colby. All hell will have to freeze over before I ever choose to visit you again." As she left the Colby Estate, wiping away the few stray tears that had emerged, she thought she heard the lone howl of a wolf. But in that moment, she refused to turn back.

✳ ✳ ✳

Jennifer busted through the living room door of her home and raced up the stairs headed for her bedroom.

She couldn't stop the tears from running down her face, and Sebastian Colby had again, gotten the better of her. But in that moment, as she collected her black candles and lit them on her bedroom floor, she swore that she would never let him claw his way into her heart again. And for that reason, Jennifer planted an unlove spell on herself.

Thanks to her emotions, the spell was powerful enough to compete with whatever spell had caused the frustrative curse that had forced their emotional rift in their families to begin with.

Never again, would she allow a Colby boy to affect her in such a way that Sebastian had done. It was a vow to close off her heart to him so she could love another.

Her current objective was Emerick. As Jennifer blew out the candles and wiped away her tears, she was startled to hear Emerick standing in her doorway.

"An unlove spell?" His eyes looked darker than she had seen them before. And instead of answering, Jennifer gravitated towards him, pulling him into an immediate kiss.

A kiss to wash away the pain that she didn't want to feel for Sebastian Colby. As they kissed, she closed her door and removed his shirt with purpose. She allowed him to remove her shirt, revealing only her black lace bra and relished the feeling of his lips against her neck. But then Emerick pulled away to catch his breath.

"We should stop," he said. "I know that something happened between you and Sebastian. We should talk about it before we do something we regret."

But Jennifer had other plans. "Stop talking, Emerick. I want to do this. Now. Okay?"

In that moment, Emerick did the only thing an incubus who hadn't had sex in centuries could do.

He held her against the door and trailed his lips from her neck to her concealed breasts, hungrily, promising to take away every ounce of pain that she had ever felt.

Every moment Jennifer and Emerick spent between the sheets not only temporarily erased Jennifer's irritating feelings for Sebastian but solidified a bond between she and Emerick.

She only prayed that the curse that had been placed on Emerick would be enough to protect him from the Morris Curse.

✳✳✳

Under the dim light of the moon, which poured in from the window, Jennifer and Emerick laid in her bed dressed in nothing more than her bedsheet.

For the first time in a very long time, Jennifer was at peace. Gone were the thoughts of Sebastian and the chaos that had been her current life.

Those thoughts had been replaced by Emerick who had the sweetest smile stretched across his face.

Peering into her eyes, he brushed her bare arm delicately with the back of his hand.

"Did you want to talk about..." he began. But Jennifer brought her finger to his lips.

"No, I don't. Because for the first time ever, I feel free. Free from the Morris Curse, free from heartbreak. Free from... Well, the entire world."

Emerick pulled her close, leaving a kiss on her forehead. "Good. Because so do I."

From her view, Jennifer noticed the swirling blue of the amulet which hung from his chest. She could've sworn she had heard a female voice calling out to her, but that would've been impossible. Surely. She lifted the blue stone into her hand to get a better look.

"What's the matter?" Emerick asked.

"I don't know. I just... I thought I heard somebody calling out to me."

"Calling out to you? Are you sure?"

Jennifer thought for a moment. Was she sure? But just as she went to doubt herself, she heard it again.

Not one voice, but numerous voices. All whispering her name in the abyss that was the amulet.

She nodded, mesmerized by the amulet. "I'm sure of it. I can't tell how many, but there are a few."

To her surprise, those very words destroyed the peace. Emerick couldn't climb out of the bed fast enough. "What's wrong?" Jennifer asked.

"You shouldn't be able to hear those voices. You need to shut them out," Emerick rushed to dress, forcing Jennifer to feel highly uncomfortable.

She shuffled to the side of the bed and pulled the blanket over her lap.

"I'm sorry, Emerick. Maybe I was just imagining things." The look of concern softened in his eyes as he knelt in front of her and rested his chin on her knee.

"Jennifer, if you're hearing their voices, I need to keep this amulet as far from you as possible. Or else I'm only putting you at risk."

"Risk of what?"

"Of them manipulating you to let them out."

"I'm stronger than I look. Are you forgetting the power I have over you?"

The confidence in her words brought a dazed look to his face. He swept his hand through her hair, kissed her and pressed her back into the bed, whispering, "how could I ever forget the power you have over me? Just give me the word and I'd swear fealty to you, forever."

His words made her blush more than she had done in a while. And why wouldn't they? She had the power to bring a demon to his knees. But before he could act on his words, Jennifer received a telepathic message from her mother. Jennifer sat bolt upright.

"Oh, goddess! Mom's home!"

TWELVE

It took barely two minutes for Jennifer and Emerick to dress, return to the living room, where they put on a movie and picked up their books, to make themselves look as if they hadn't been up to much at all.

Within the next breath, Marian entered through the front door. But the woman was highly preoccupied with the visitors that were waiting outside.

"Jennifer? It seems you have some visitors." Jennifer and Emerick peered up from their books, confused.

"Visitors, mom?"

From the doorway, Marian pointed outside. "Out there, dear. Please tell them it's a little late to be calling in at this hour. Even for Sebastian."

Jennifer gestured for Emerick to wait in the living room as she passed her mother, headed for outside. Sure enough, Sebastian and Marco were waiting in the front yard with a peculiar mixture of animosity and confusion lingering between them.

Hesitantly, Jennifer stepped outside into the brisk night air, closing the door behind her.

"Sebastian, Marco? What are you guys doing here?"

Sebastian stepped forward, confidently showing who the alpha of the two was. "I wanted to tell you I'm sorry, Jennifer. I never should've said what I said. Please, forgive me."

"No, Jennifer. Don't listen to him," Marco interjected. "Normally, I'm not one to speak up in front of Sebastian. But you can't choose him. I love you. I was even willing to tie up the school nurse for you."

"He, what...?" Sebastian exclaimed. "Dude, how could..."

"...It was to show Jen just how much I love her. Nurse Violet was trying to..."

"...Seriously, Marco?" Jennifer interjected. "You need to go and untie her, right now! Your mother is the goddam Deputy Sheriff!"

"I'll go," Sebastian decided. "Been cleaning this guy's mess for a long time, may as well do this too. Jennifer, come with me and we'll talk along the way." Drawing a full conclusion of the scene, Jennifer remembered what Ambrose had said about the concept of groupies and realized she now had to suffer the consequences.

"No, Sebastian. That won't be necessary. You guys just..."

"…Is everything okay out here?" Emerick's voice came from the doorway, forcing both Sebastian and Marco to go on the offense.

"Why do you smell like him?" Sebastian asked.

Jennifer couldn't answer that question entirely. She needed to get back to the crisis at hand. "Never mind that. I need to go and help Violet. The two of you, go home."

"I'm not leaving you," Sebastian snapped. "That guy's a demon. I don't trust him."

"A demon? Then I won't leave you either, Jennifer." Marco said.

Jennifer could've slapped Sebastian for revealing the truth out in the open. But now was not the time.

Instead, she told all three to wait for her outside and returned inside to speak with her mother.

"Mom, I need to go to the school."

"At this hour? Jenny, it's almost midnight."

Jennifer nodded. Pleaded. "You see, something happened and now Nurse Violet is..."

"Seriously, Jennifer? How many times have I had to tell you to just use magic?" Marian snapped her fingers, midsentence. "There, she should be free, now."

"Wait, what?"

"Now, why don't you tell me what's really going on?"

Jennifer froze. How was she supposed to tell her mother that she had infected herself with the incubus curse and was currently making groupies out of her high school peers? Suddenly, loud sirens could be heard approaching from outside.

"Oh, goddess!" Marian exclaimed, opening the door wider to get a view of the yard. "You just had to bring the police home to our door, didn't you Jennifer?"

For the first time in a long time, Jennifer witnessed the fury that she rarely saw in her mother. She followed Marian outside where two patrol cars pulled up. While Jennifer joined Emerick, Sebastian, and Marco, Marian went to address Sheriff Mike.

"I'm assuming they found the nurse," Emerick said. But it was the look of sheer concern on Sebastian's face as he focused his hearing on Marian and Sheriff Mike's conversation, that told Jennifer he had heard something more dire.

Sebastian glared at Emerick, speechless, as Sheriff Mike, Deputy Olivia, and Ambrose – who looked as if his entire world had just been shattered – approached them.

"Emerick Gremory, you're under arrest for the murder of Aisha Prescott." Sheriff Mike said, while taking out his handcuffs. He approached Emerick – who didn't fight him. "You have the right to remain silent…" As the Sheriff continued to read Emerick his rights, Jennifer struggled to comprehend just what the sheriff had said. There was no way in hell that Aisha could be dead. Nor was there any way that Emerick could've been the one responsible.

Her world was spinning.

She began to zone out – and as she did – an ear-piercing ring drowned out all other noise. Just as she felt as if her feet were about to give out from under her, Sebastian pulled her away from Emerick as the Sheriff began to lead Emerick to the car.

There was a hurricane in Jennifer's mind. Using all her strength, she pushed out of Sebastian's arms and ran after Sheriff Mike. "There has to be some mistake," she demanded. "Emerick has been with me. He can't have killed Aisha."

Sheriff Mike shook his head. "I'm sorry, Jennifer. We saw the footage. Even Ambrose couldn't believe what he saw."

Jennifer stood in Emerick's way so the Sheriff couldn't put him into the car and continued to plead Emerick's case, "tell them, Emerick. Tell them you didn't do it."

"It won't make a difference," Emerick said. "I doubt they'll believe me."

Jennifer raced over to Ambrose, who looked just as heartbroken as she was. "You did it, didn't you?! How could you kill my best friend and blame it on your own damn brother, You're a monster!"

She hit him and hit him but was pulled away again by Sebastian, where she crumbled in grief.

"Boys, we should take you home," Olivia said to Marco and Sebastian. But thanks to that damn groupie side effect, neither would leave Jennifer's side. "Marco Henderson, get in that car right now!" Olivia shouted at her son. "After that stunt you pulled on Nurse Violet, you're lucky she isn't pressing charges!"

"I'm not leaving Jennifer's side," he argued. To Jennifer's stunned surprise, Ambrose placed his hand on Marco's shoulder and spoke boldly, with that same cool tone he would use while singing. "Go home, kid. Listen to your mom."

On those words, Marco shrugged off whatever compulsion Jennifer had over him and left with his mother. But it was the odd look Ambrose gave Sebastian when he tried to remove his compulsion that was peculiar to say the least. Almost as if Ambrose saw no groupie compulsion in Sebastian whatsoever. Ambrose shrugged it off, then climbed into the same patrol car as Emerick and the Sheriff.

As the lights to the patrol cars disappeared down the dark street, Jennifer was left with Marian, Sebastian and the gut-wrenchingly unbelievable news that Emerick had just been arrested for the death of her best friend.

The death of Aisha.

✳ ✳ ✳

As Emerick sat in the back of the patrol car, he questioned himself of how he could be in that situation. Externally, Sheriff Mike was bringing up light conversation, while Ambrose said nothing at all. Emerick's thoughts of Jennifer crying out on his behalf merely added to the guilt he felt. He had promised himself he wouldn't pull her into his mess. Now she was in the sheer thick of it with him.

Emerick tried to think back to the last time he had seen Aisha.

It was at the school. Jennifer had left them alone in the corridor for only a few minutes. He had been feeling off again and then... That switch had been flicked.

Blurred images of warped memories flashed through his mind. Almost as if it had been a lifetime ago. Only it hadn't been. It was only a few days ago.

Emerick had kissed Aisha in that hall and consumed her soul. But that was impossible. He would've never done something so cruel.

So, why was the memory there at all?

Another blurred image flashed through his mind. In that memory he was making out with Emma Bryce. Again, he swallowed her soul.

There was a girl in the park. A girl on the beach. So many different girls all in different towns.

As the gut-wrenching thoughts took hold, he glanced down at the amulet at his neck. It was glowing brighter than ever.

Was that the reason for the memories? Or was he truly the killer with a severe case of selective amnesia?

THIRTEEN

With Marian pacing the living room, Jennifer explained the entire situation through heartfelt tears, to she and Sebastian from her position on the couch. From the part about the spell that had granted Jennifer the ability to create groupies, to the part where she had created an unlove spell on Sebastian.

Knowing that the truth of her sleeping with Emerick would only anger Marian more, Jennifer chose to leave that part out.

"Seriously, Jennifer? I can't believe you made a spell to stop yourself from... from feeling for me?" Sebastian vented from beside her. He was beyond mad, but Jennifer didn't regret her actions.

"What did you expect? I wanted to be free from that god-awful curse that our families are enslaved to."

"Did you ever for one minute stop to think about what I want?"

"Actually, I did. Think about it. Every man who loves a Morris Woman dies. They're cursed. So, I saved you from meeting your untimely death."

"Oh, come on, Jennifer! I would rather die knowing we loved one another, than live a long life with somebody I don't love. Why can't you see that?"

"Well, that's your fault, Sebastian. You got Daniella preg…"

"SILENCE!" Marian yelled for probably the first time in Jennifer's entire life, drawing their attention. "Now, you've both made a lot of mistakes. Neither of you are innocent. But that incubus who has just been arrested did not commit those crimes."

"But Sheriff Mike saw the footage," Sebastian said.

"I know what he said. But that demon is not a killer," Marian said before taking a moment to register. "I can't believe I just said that. It goes against everything I've ever believed in, but *that* demon is not responsible for the murders of those girls."

"Who do you think it was?" Jennifer asked.

"I don't know, but we're going to find out. You two, follow me." On those words, Marian led Jennifer and Sebastian up to her summoning room.

Just as the older Morris Witch raised her hand above the crystal ball, she stopped and focused her attention on Sebastian.

"Please tell your father you're here helping with an investigation, Sebastian. He's about to call."

As she said those words, Sebastian's phone rang. Tongue in cheek, he answered it and quickly did as she had instructed. Once he ended the call he asked, "how did you know that would happen?"

"The two of you are so naïve to even think you're the only generation to be linked by that damn curse. And why I had hoped you might've broken it. I guess we'll leave that work to your children then, shall we?"

Jennifer rolled her eyes. "Seriously mom. I'm not planning on having children for a very..." But Marian gave her a frightening look, before abruptly changing the subject. "Now, Jennifer, raise your hand over the ball. When was the last time you spoke with Aisha in person?"

"It was..."

Jennifer thought back to the moment she had left Aisha with Emerick and had gone to speak with Sebastian. That very conversation that had ended in them kissing thanks to her need for energy. "Before I went to talk to Sebastian about the wolf attack."

She looked to Sebastian, who pursed his lips together knowing exactly what she had been thinking.

"You remember the wolf attack, right Seb...?"

"...Shh." Marian hushed as she stared into the ball. "You're supposed to be going to a party tomorrow, right?"

"Ah..."
"The killer will be there."

"Can you tell who it is?" Sebastian asked.

Marian focused harder on the everchanging colored smoke in the ball.

"It has many faces. Many forms. And it's hunger. That hunger is horrible. So horrible. You'll need to trap it. We need to send it to hell."

Jennifer thought for a moment. "What if we use Emerick's amulet?"

"His amulet?"

"Yes, it's literally a prison for demon souls. He uses it so he doesn't need to devour innocent souls."

Marian considered the thought and then asked, "that is the amulet you used to preform your protection spell, isn't it?"

"That's the one."

"Good idea. The two of you can collect it from Emerick tomorrow, while I distract Mike. But you'll need to be very careful. We don't need to unleash hell on earth all over again."

That last sentence filled Jennifer and Sebastian with many unanswered questions.

"What do you mean *again*?" Sebastian asked.

"You should ask your father about that one.

He tells it better than I do. Now, it is very late. You should go home, Sebastian. We will see you tomorrow. Jennifer, you can see him out."

✻ ✻ ✻

As Jennifer saw Sebastian to the front door, she merely counted down the seconds before he started with his line of questions. "How are you doing with everything?" he asked.

"What's there to say? Tonight's been rough. First there was you, then Emerick... and now all this with Aisha. I feel like my life is falling apart. She was my best friend. I loved her."

"She felt the same way about you. I can still remember the day you two met. Damn, that girl had sass."

Jennifer giggled. "Wait, how do you remember the day we..."

"It was when we were dating. We were fighting about something silly, and this new girl came in and was all like 'you guys sound like a married couple' and you just lost it because..."

"...Because that's what we were arguing about. You had just told me you'd marry me, and I was upset because it would've meant I'd lose you to the curse."

"Man, we were just kids then. I can't believe she's gone."

Jennifer nodded. But her motion of agreement brought out her tears of misery.

Sebastian pulled her into his arms and they both cried over the loss of an old friend. Amidst her despair, Jennifer was glad to have her oldest and dearest friend by her side, regardless of their feelings for each other. "It's okay," he whispered into her. "Nothing will stop me from being there for you. Not even death and I mean that."

Jennifer cherished those words. And when her tears finally subsided, she mustered her strength to pull out of his arms. Sebastian wiped her tears away with his thumbs. "I'll be here first thing tomorrow, okay?"

"Thanks. I appreciate it."

Solemnly, she watched as he climbed into his red jaguar and disappeared down the road, before heading back inside to find her mother waiting with a conflicted expression on her face.

"If you ask me the real curse that plagues our families is that we can't bring ourselves to be happy even just for a moment."

"What do you mean?" Jennifer asked.

As quickly as the thought appeared, Marian shook it off. "Never mind. I really liked Aisha. The girl didn't take crap from anybody. How are you coping?"

"I'll cope better when we find her killer. I'm going to bed," Jennifer bypassed Marian just as the older woman received a strange vibe about her daughter.

One that she couldn't quite put her finger on. She brushed it off. "Goodnight, Jennifer."

✳ ✳ ✳

The next morning, Sebastian and Marian stood around Jennifer's bed struggling to wake her up from a very deep sleep.

"Wake up, Jenny," Marian called out. "We're heading to the Sheriff's Department now!"

"Do you think maybe it's that succubus spell she mentioned?" Sebastian asked.

Marian waved her hand over her sleeping daughter. Her hand stopped once it hovered over Jennifer's stomach and Marian's entire body froze.

"Son of a bitch!"

"Miss Morris?"

"Oh, it's that curse all right! That goddam demon got my daughter pregnant so now she's going to need to feast on souls like they're a multivitamin. You need to kiss her."

"Ah, what?"

"You heard me, she's pregnant and she's dealing with that awful incubus-succubus curse. Go on, do it!"

Sebastian backed towards the door. "Miss Morris. Jennifer and I aren't together. I can't just..."

"Oh, that never stopped you before!"

"Well, then. What about the fact that if I kiss her, she could kill me?"

"It's either that, or she dies."

Sebastian considered the option for merely a second, before he knelt beside Jennifer on the bed.

"You can hate me later." He pressed his lips against hers and at first, nothing happened.

Soon, he felt Jennifer return the kiss. Once again, it was perfect and forced him to wonder why she refused to be with him, until he felt an overwhelming weakness take over his entire body.

And then he felt like the soul of the wolf that shared his body was trying to take over. He needed to pull away. Needed to break the connection, but at the same time, he didn't want to.

He only wanted Jennifer.

The moment he felt like he was done for, Jennifer broke their embrace. And she did so, violently, flinging him across the room. "Seriously, Sebastian? What the hell?! I could've killed you!"

Sebastian felt weaker than he had ever felt but defended his case regardless.

"It was either that or…"

"…You took advantage of me while I was sleeping, Sebastian, that's just wrong! How could you?!"

"He was doing what he needed to do so you wouldn't die, Jennifer." Marian broke in. "You're pregnant. And you're going to need to feast on souls, frequently now. I asked Sebastian to do the honors. And don't worry, I wouldn't have let you kill him. Now, get up. We needed to be at the Sheriff's department half an hour ago. Come on, Sebastian. We'll meet her downstairs."

As Sebastian followed Marian into the kitchen, he was baffled by the thought.

How could Jennifer be pregnant?

Did incubuses... incubi... Could they even conceive? Regardless of the notion, it meant that both he and Jennifer would soon be parents, and while that was amazing, the part that broke his heart, was that he had always wanted to start his family with her.

FOURTEEN

Marian escorted Jennifer and Sebastian to the Sheriff's Department and while the older Morris woman spoke with the Sheriff, Jennifer struggled to comprehend just what her mother had revealed. "Are you alright?" Sebastian asked, forcing Jennifer to raise her head and then lower it again in a single nod.

"I think so. I don't understand how I could be pregnant. Emerick's an incubus. I don't think they can even have children."

"I know. Just so you know, you can always depend on me to help you out. With anything, really."

"Oh, Mike!" Marian's raised voice interrupted. "I know what he is, and I know what he is capable of. I may not agree with his sort, but I know he's not a killer."

"I'm sorry, Marian, but I've had the same argument with his brother. The video footage shows his face as clear as day."

"Pfft! Science strikes again! Show me this footage."

"I'd rather not. We're talking about the confidential graphic imaging of..."

Marian flicked her hair, brought her hand to the Sheriff's shoulder and softened her tone to a more seductive one. "Now, Mike. I won't be showing the children. I just want to make my own assessment so we can find the true killer. Can you fault me for that?" Sheriff Mike blinked once. Then twice. And then to all their relief, he caved and showed Marian his laptop. Jennifer and Sebastian watched with great curiosity as Marian witnessed the silent video, voicing her remarks with a tone that didn't sound even half as traumatized as it should have.

"Oh goddess. The poor girl. Oh my. What a way to go." Once the video had finished, Sheriff Mike closed the computer to debrief with her.

"You don't sound shocked, Miss Morris."

"Why would I be? This isn't my first rodeo. Don't you remember that nonsense at Barrett Manor eighteen years ago?"

"Oh, right! Yes. Does your daughter know?"

"No, she…"

"…Mom! Was it Emerick in the video or not?" Jennifer exclaimed, getting to her feet.

"While it sure looks that way…" Jennifer's entire world shattered. She was sure that Emerick wasn't the murderer. Still, Marian continued. "I don't buy it. Would you mind letting Jennifer and Sebastian go in and speak with him. I assure you, they're as trustworthy as they come."

Sheriff Mike considered her request and thanks to that compelling smile on Marian's face, he just couldn't say 'no'.

✳✳✳

Jennifer and Sebastian took their seats across the table from Emerick, who was still in handcuffs. Though, this time he was dressed in grey prison attire and his eyes were bloodshot.

Seeing him in such a way, broke Jennifer's heart, but her fiercest struggle was on how to reveal the news to him regarding the child that she was carrying.

"How are you doing?" she asked him.

"I've been better," he said. "They're accusing me of all the murders across Richmont. Ambrose left this morning. I don't think he believes me."

"We're going to get you out of here, Emerick. I promise. But we need to borrow the amulet."

"My amulet? Why?"

"My mother thinks we may be able to track down the killer and then trap them within the stone. I don't know how, but she believes they're going to be at the party tonight."

"I can't let you do that, Jennifer."

"Why not?" Sebastian asked, irritated.

"Why do you think?" Emerick scoffed. "It's the only way to keep me from devouring the souls of the innocents."

Before Jennifer could give her argument, Sebastian leaned forward and gripped Emerick's collar. "Have you even considered for just one moment the situation that Jennifer is in? Because of you and that damn curse you infected her with, she's literally a liability to not only herself but everybody around her. So, hand over the damn amulet now!"

"Sebastian," Jennifer argued. "I'm fine."

"No, you're not. You almost died this morning. We're lucky that I was there to..."

Catching the drift of their conversation, Emerick cut in. "What happened this morning?"

"Nothing happened," Jennifer snapped. "I'm fine."

"No, you're not," Sebastian argued, before turning his frustration back to Emerick.

"For your information, she almost died, and we were lucky I was there to give her mouth-to-mouth resuscitation or not only would we have lost Jennifer, but you would've lost your child too."

Jennifer dropped her head into her arms and groaned. "Seriously, Sebastian?! That wasn't your news to tell."

"Oh yeah? Like you were just waiting for the opportunity to tell him? He deserved to know."

Reminded by the news that her mother had revealed to him in relation to Daniella's pregnancy, Jennifer knew she couldn't fault him for that.

But it didn't stop her from being angry at him. She raised her head and glared at Sebastian.

"So, what...? That makes us even? You're so frustrating, did you know that?"

"You guys, stop!" Emerick said. "Jennifer, is that true? Are you really pregnant?"

Jennifer sighed in defeat. "As you saw with Daniella, my mother can tell from day one when a girl is pregnant. She can also tell who the father is just by sense alone. Apparently, after last night... You and I..."

"...But that's not possible," Emerick replied. "My kind can't have children. We devour souls, we can't procreate."

"That's what I thought too. But maybe we created a loophole with the spell."

For a bitterly long moment, there was nothing but silence as Emerick took in the news.

Thanks to the expression on his face, how Emerick was feeling about the news was impossible to determine.

"Say something, please," she whispered.

Emerick swallowed the saliva that came up in his throat, shuffled in his seat and finally revealed what looked to be a smile.

"It's just... it's going to take some time to process... Here, take the amulet, I'll ask Ambrose for some assistance for myself." With his wrists cuffed, Emerick removed the amulet from his neck and handed it to her. "Every time you feel the exhaustion taking over, rub the amulet. Just promise me, you'll be careful with it."

"Of course, I promise. And don't worry. We'll get you out of here."

As Jennifer fastened the amulet to her neck, her eyes flashed from green to blue and then back to green again. She kissed Emerick 'goodbye' and led Sebastian towards the exits.

But before they could leave, Emerick addressed Sebastian.

"I need you to promise me, that you'll look after her. If anything happens..."

Sebastian turned back. "I've been making that promise since we were children. It's nothing new to me."

Emerick nodded, solemnly. "Thank you."

✳✳✳

As Emerick was led back to his cell, by Sheriff Mike, he struggled with the very news that Sebastian had cornered him with.

The very thought that he had fathered a child with Jennifer was crippling. And not just because he had given up on that dream centuries ago.

For over a millennia Emerick had grown accustomed to the fact that incubi couldn't produce children.

But then, why would they want to? No parent would want to subject their child to the curse of soul devouring.

But now, he had done just that. And to make matters worse, he had given Jennifer the one thing he felt was responsible for the murders.

He was sure that whatever demon had taken possession of it, had the ability to control whoever wore it. Those theories were only founded by the vague memories he continued to see in his mind.

He had seen the footage of Aisha's death in the empty school corridor. There was no doubt about it. She had died at his hands.

However, what had caused him to do it and why, were still mysteries. And it was it for those reasons that Emerick needed to trust Sebastian with not only the life of Jennifer, but also the life of their unborn child.

He just hoped he was right in his assumptions that Sebastian would go to any length to uphold that that promise which included the very depths of hell.

❋ ❋ ❋

Later that day, Marian ran a thorough assessment over the amulet in her summoning room as it adorned Jennifer's neck.

"This is very fascinating," she hummed.

"What?" Jennifer asked.

"I've never seen this kind of magic before. It's almost as if it was actually crafted in hell. Did Emerick tell you who made it? Better yet, who cursed him?"

"It was so long ago he couldn't really remember. He just said that this was one of his oldest possessions."

"They must've used a Forget spell on him. Maybe you should consult with his brother. He might be able to offer a little more insight. Delve into his memories if you have to. We need these answers before you even risk tracking the killer."

"I'll head to Barrett Manor as soon as I leave here."

"Barrett Manor? Jennifer, no!"

"But that's where he's staying. That's also where the party is being held."

Marian stepped backwards. The fear that was in her eyes terrified Jennifer.

But Marian seemed to be silently considering their options. Alas, there were none.

"Of course, the party had to be held there. Jennifer, you must promise me that you will be careful at Barrett Manor. Don't go into any rooms alone. Don't devour a soul in the house, no matter what. Take Sebastian with you. Take every precaution you possibly..."

"...Relax, mom. I've got it covered. I know how to protect myself."

Marian breathed out. But she wasn't relieved or even remotely convinced.

"I don't trust that place. Or that older brother, even if you are immune to his seductions."

Jennifer nodded but looked to change the subject. "What type of reading do you get from these souls?"

"The souls in that prison... The stronger ones are as Emerick said. Vile, horrible demons. You're best being careful with them. But then, there's the souls who appear frightened by all that surrounds them. I can't get a reading because it's as if the poor dears are hiding away from me. Though, they could just be trying to trick us."

"Can we free them?"

"Not without freeing the demons. Do not listen to them Jennifer. Only use the amulet as intended and leave it at that. Do you understand me?"

Jennifer nodded. She understood her mother loud and clear.

But she couldn't help but feel for the poor souls who were trapped amongst the hellish prison that adorned her neck. It made her think of Emerick stuck in that cold cell, alone, waiting for her to find the true killer.

In that moment Jennifer made a vow that she would do anything to stop the killer, free Emerick and avenge Aisha, Emma Bryce and all the other girls who had ever fallen prey to the monster. Assuming her mother was done with her assessment, Jennifer asked, "are we finished here?"

But Marian waved her fingers in another circular motion at the amulet.

"Now we are. I just laced that amulet with an extra seal. Just promise me, you'll only devour the souls as needed and never within that house. Do you promise?"

"I promise."

With nothing left to discuss, Jennifer joined Sebastian, who was waiting in the living room.

"We're heading to Barrett Manor," she said, only for his eyes to go wide.

Sebastian was frightened of so few things, but remarkably, Barrett Manor was one of those things. Reading his expression, Jennifer found her purse and headed to the door asking, "what's the deal with that place anyway? I hear it's surrounded in bad magic. It literally terrifies my mom."

"She never told you?" he asked as they left the house and approached his car.

"Nope."

"That place is rumored to contain a gateway to hell. I asked my dad about it after what the Sheriff said this morning and apparently, there was some big near apocalypse before we were born. Mortals were hunted by demons, and it was up to our kind to save them. My dad still suffers from PTSD."

"Shit!"

"I know, right?"

They climbed into the car and Sebastian took the main road through Richmont headed for the large house that loomed on the highest mountain peak of town.

"Does anybody know about me and Daniella yet?" he asked after a long bout of silence.

"Not that I know. Why?"

"News tends to spread fast in Richmont."

Jennifer offered him a sympathetic smile. "Have you heard from her?"

"Not a word since we broke up. It's not like I want us to get back together or anything. It's just..."

"...I get it. I'm in that complicated having-a-baby-but-separated-from-the-other-parent-boat too. We'll get through it together, alright?"

Sebastian nodded then took a left turn as the car took the winding road up the hill. "Scared yet?" he asked, referring to the large building at the top of the hill, which looked creepy even in the daylight.

"Me? Never? But I do need you to pull over for a second."

"Why?"

"I promised my mom I'd use the amulet before we entered the house. She's afraid I'll unleash a demon."

"You're braver than I am," Sebastian said, pulling to the side of the road.

He waited as Jennifer peered down at the amulet. Again, she heard those whispers calling out her name.

For a moment, she thought she could hear Aisha's voice. But then again, demons had a way of fooling people, she knew it couldn't be her best friend.

Ignoring the voices, Jennifer rubbed the amulet and saw what could only be compared to the black smoke she had seen in the crystal ball.

It emerged from the blue stone and slowly lingered towards her face. As if on impulse, she breathed it in and allowed the smoke to invigorate her very senses. The soul entered through her mouth and nose, causing a surge of ecstasy to course through her veins, providing an overwhelmingly pleasurable experience. Once the smoke settled in the pit of her stomach leaving her breathless, she turned to Sebastian with a smile that left her dazed.

"Damn, that was better than sex."

Sebastian seemed to not know whether to laugh or take offense to her comment. Instead, he bit down on his lower lip, pulled back onto the road, and spoke under his breath. "That's only because we haven't done it in a while."

While he spoke it quietly, Jennifer had still heard it and her response surprised even herself. "That can always be changed, dear wolf."

"Excuse me?"

Jennifer stared in horror. "I... ahh... that wasn't me. That was..."

Sebastian stopped the car and studied her face. "Wait, your eyes are blue, Jennifer."

"What are you talking about? My eyes are green."

"No. I know that. But your eyes have turned blue." He brought his nose to her neck.

"You smell different too. I think that soul did something to you." As Jennifer felt the crazy energy that the soul continued to ignite in her body, she realized just how hard Emerick must've been battling to keep his urges at bay.

There was something about having Sebastian's face so close to her neck that made her struggle with her own self-control. But she forced herself to resist.

When Sebastian pulled away, he was lost in thought. "I think we need to abort the plan. Give the amulet back to Emerick and..."

"No!" Jennifer snapped. "We need to do this. We need to prove that Emerick didn't commit those murders and avenge all those girls. Please, Sebastian."

"Are you sure?" Despite those strong urges to take advantage of Sebastian in that very car, Jennifer was very sure that justice was what she wanted. "Positive. We should speak with Ambrose now. Maybe he can help."

On her word, Sebastian continued the drive to the top of the hill. She could sense his hesitation. And she should've listened to her intuition which was begging her to listen to him.

Instead, it was her determination to seek justice that forced her to go to Barrett Manor ready to make the worst mistake of her life.

FIFTEEN

The first thing Jennifer noticed when she stepped foot in Barrett Manor was just how luxurious the place must've been over a hundred years ago. It was no wonder the mortals believed it to be a vampire's lair, no other description could do it justice. They were standing in what seemed to be a great hall. The thick burgundy drapes had been pulled open to invite in the piercing sunlight. Elegant chandeliers hung in each large room. Gothic-styled furniture and red velvet rugs lined the mahogany floors. Several feet from the front entrance, was a wooden stairwell headed for upstairs.

The luxurious interior reminded Jennifer of the vision that she had received and every fiber of her being told her to turn and leave. But the demon soul that was coursing through her veins relished the thought of being there and she couldn't turn back. It felt physically impossible. As if she was trapped within her own body, forced to take actions that she didn't want to take.

"Why would he choose here of all places?" Sebastian asked. His tone strained.

"The guy's a demon," Jennifer replied. "Clearly, he feels right at home."

"Of course, he would feel at home. We're on the cusp of hell."

"It'll be alright. I promise," Jennifer said hoping he would buy her lie.

Remembering why they were there, she headed up the steps in search of the demon of the house, with Sebastian trailing right behind. "Ambrose?" she called, unsure if he could hear her.

Once she reached the landing, they were standing in a large corridor filled with doors on either side. They continued right.

"Ambrose?" she called out again, listening carefully. They heard a noise in one of the rooms to the left and ventured towards it.

Jennifer opened the door immediately and was appalled by the sight. "Eww! Gross!"

She tried to avert her eyes at seeing Ambrose naked on his bed surrounded by approximately five men and women roughly in their early twenties. Sebastian burst into laughter.

"We totally should've knocked," he chuckled.

"Yes, you should've," Ambrose said, draping a sheet around his waist as he made his way towards them. "What are you doing here?"

Cautiously, Jennifer removed her hand and opposed him.

"I need answers. I want to find the killer and free your brother. But clearly, you have just confirmed my suspicions that it was you."

"Not this again, Jennifer. I'm not the monster you keep painting me out to be."

"Well, judging by the fact that you're having some wild orgy while your brother is rotting in prison tells me otherwise."

Ambrose looked to Sebastian then back to Jennifer as if trying to find the right words to admit defeat. "Seriously?" he scoffed. "I'm here because there's nothing else, I can do for him. He's my goddam brother! The last thing I want is for him to be locked away in that prison, but all evidence points to him."

"Bullshit!"

"Does your mother know you talk like that?"

"Cut the crap, Ambrose. You know Emerick. He can't have done it. He hates the thought of devouring innocents..."

"...That's what I thought too until I saw the footage. Aisha was your friend. You should be remembering her, not trying to pin the evidence onto somebody else. Now go home. I don't need some schoolgirl ruining my pity party."

Jennifer turned to Sebastian in disbelief, then remembered the party and turned back to the sex-crazed demon.

"Speaking of parties, my mother did a reading and said the killer will be here, tonight."

"Impossible. I'm cancelling the party," Ambrose said. "I don't have a lead guitarist."

"You can't cancel!"

"Watch me, now go away. And take your little guard dog with you."

And with that, Ambrose slammed the door in their faces, forcing Jennifer to grumble. "I hate that guy. It's like I have no power over him."

A smile spread across Sebastian's face. "That really must suck, huh?" She got his joke and while it annoyed her, it also gave her an idea. Well, it was less her idea than it was the idea of the demon coursing through her veins. But she knew she possessed the Morris strength to make it work. Jennifer lifted the amulet in her hand.

"What are you doing?" Sebastian cried, grabbing her hand to stop her.

"What does it look like? I'm building up the power to make him listen to me. He *will* have that party and we *will* catch the killer tonight."

"But you promised your mother you wouldn't do it in this house." Jennifer brought her hand to his cheek, mustering her Morris Charm.

"You do trust me, don't you, Sebastian?"

He tried to nudge her away but couldn't.

"Normally, yes. But..."

She grazed his chin with her fingertips, giggled and spoke with a tone that went beyond the Morris Charm. "Well, you need to trust me now, wolf. Ambrose and I go way back. I have this covered."

As she pulled her hand away from his chin, he was left with a docile look, giving Jennifer the chance to rub the amulet and draw out another soul. Instead of black smoke, there was a foggy red soul. Alluring, seductive and promising an even more ecstatic high than the last soul had delivered. She inhaled it and let it consume her entire body.

The high was insatiable, and her eyes were even bluer than they had been before. They could only be compared to the amulet itself. But it was the smile on her face that resembled anything but the Jennifer that Sebastian had come to know.

"This will be fun," she said to Sebastian, who had managed to break free from his trancelike state. "Now, be a good dog and stand guard. Okay?"

"Excuse me?!" Sebastian shot back. Jennifer opened the door and stormed into the room with a newfound confidence, immediately breaking up Ambrose's intimate soiree.

Again, Ambrose draped the sheet around his waist and stood to oppose her.

"What are you doing, Jennifer? You need to leave right now before I arrest you for trespassing!"

"You're not a real cop, Ambrose," Jennifer cooed. "But I'd love to see you *try*. We could have some fun. You be the bad cop... I be the sexy demon in need of a good exorcism. What do you say?"

Taking in Jennifer's façade, Ambrose froze. He examined her eyes and then noticed the amulet at her neck. "Oh no, what have you done?"

Jennifer smiled. Again, that eerie smile.

"I did nothing. Your brother was the one who was scared you would hurt her. Their spell gave me to her. But it feels kind of fitting living and breathing in the body of a Morris Witch. She has a lure that reaches beyond that of young girls. What do you think?"

The demon grabbed his hands and ran them up her torso leading them towards her breasts.

"You love that, don't you, Ambrose? Brings back so many old memories. Doesn't it?"

He was nothing more than a slave to his own desire. "I have a bed right there, what do you say?"

She removed his hands. "Not now. My loyal soldier. You're having that party, tonight. You need to prepare."

She kissed him and he was putty in her hands. She inhaled his energy, but only enough to savor her thirst, before pulling away again.

As she broke the connection, he fell to his knees and kissed her feet in passionate submission.

His kiss continued to trail up her leg, daring to go further.

"You have my word, duchess. Whatever you want, you need only say the word."

"Glad we agree." Jennifer turned her attention to Ambrose's groupies who sat silently on the bed.

Two handsome men and three beautiful women. "You obey me now. Do you understand?"

As nothing more than mindless slaves, they joined Ambrose on their knees in submission.

"What is your name?" the naked, blond woman asked.

Jennifer smiled. "It's Gremory. Now, I will need all of you to ensure that this party will be a night that nobody will ever forget. Do you understand?"

Gremory, as she preferred to be called, turned on her heels, ready to leave. But Ambrose trailed after her. "Where are you going, duchess? Let me follow you. Please."

"That won't be necessary, Ambrose. I am going to free your brother from that dank, cell. He will be needed for tonight's ritual."

"Ritual?"

"When have I ever revealed all my cards?" Without another word, Gremory left the room, motioning for Sebastian to follow.

When they were in his car, Sebastian took a moment to process his thoughts as he thumbed with his key.

He seemed to be fighting a tiresome battle with his own self-control which Gremory noticed.

"Dear wolf, what troubles you?"

"You're not Jennifer."

"Oh no. Of course, I'm not. I'm better."

"What do you want with her?"

Gremory peered out the window at the large house, then turned back to face him.

"You need not worry about that now. All I ask is that you take us to free Emerick."

"Are you crazy? No!"

"Oh, you need not be jealous, wolf. I simply need him for a ritual. Just as I need you."

Sebastian crossed his arms and shook his head. Ignorant to her request.

"I might not possess the power to lure men, but this vessel does. I have ways of making you listen. Surely, you remember that little compulsion I used on you in that house, I can certainly use it again. And trust me, you'll find it very worthwhile."

Sebastian peered down at Gremory's hands that were trailing up her thighs, towards the hemline of her black skirt, suggestively. No, not Gremory's hands and thighs. They belonged to Jennifer. But that was the weakness that Gremory could exploit in him.

While Sebastian was beyond tempted, he shook off the thought like one would shake off the cold while standing in front of a warm fireplace.

"Alright, fine," he said, starting up the car. "We'll get Emerick, but I have no idea how we're going to free..."

"...Leave that to me."

SIXTEEN

Sebastian pulled into the parking lot of the Sheriff's Department and turned off the ignition. He knew he was making a big mistake by following along with the demon. But he didn't know how to break the compulsion. He was normally an alpha. But whenever it came to Jennifer, he could never seem to break free. Now, his situation was worse than it had ever been. That demon, that *Gremory* as he had heard her reveal earlier, continued to wave the temptation of Jennifer around like a delicious slice of pizza. A pizza that smelled like lavender, as weird as the metaphor sounded.

Though this time, that lavender scent was tainted with something potent. He had smelled that same poison on Emerick in the past. Sebastian peered up at the *thing* posing as Jennifer.

"Well, we're here," he said.

"I can see that. Are you not escorting me?"

Sebastian shook his head. "No, but I can keep the car running."

At least if she wasn't near him, he could use his phone to call his dad or even Marian.

But Gremory was adamant. "I want you with me, wolf."

"I said *no*."

But she wouldn't buy it.

She took his hand, possessing a physical strength he had no chance of breaking free from and brought it to her thigh.

"Sebastian," she cooed. "I know you want to touch me. I can sense the need in you. I felt it when we kissed before I went back to Emerick."

As his hand was guided up past the hemline of her dress, he thought back to the kiss he shared with Jennifer. To when he had told her that he loved her. Had Gremory really been possessing Jennifer's body since before then? How had he not seen it? Or maybe that thing was reading her thoughts. Could demons really do that?

As he felt his fingers make contact with the flesh between Jennifer's legs, it took all the strength he had to concede to the demon's will.

"Fine! I'll go with you. Just let go of me."

The moment he gave in, she released his hand, forcing him to rip it back with such ferocity.

Gremory smiled. "Good dog. It's so sweet to see how loyal you are. It certainly makes her wonder why the two of you broke up."

As Sebastian slammed opened his door, her words gave him pause. Was the demon lying? How could Jennifer have forgotten? They only ever broke up because she was terrified of the thought of him having to die.

Then there was the fact that he had his doubts about the wolf thing, but that was never a big issue.

Maybe the Gremory demon was playing with his head. Brushing off the thought, Sebastian followed Gremory into the Sheriff's Department.

"We're here to release Emerick from prison," Gremory said to Deputy Olivia Henderson.

"We can't do that, Jennifer. Not without proof."

While Sebastian had seen that coming, he hadn't expected to see what Gremory did next.

She brought her hand to Olivia's chin, stared into her dark eyes and said, "oh, I'm all the proof you need, Deputy Henderson. You see, I committed the murders. But you're not going to arrest me. Instead, you're going release Emerick and come to Barrett Manor tonight. Oh, and bring Marco. He's sure to love it, too."

Olivia blinked twice before submitting to Gremory's will. "It will be done."

After the Deputy headed towards the holding cells with the keys, Sebastian gasped.

"What the hell? How did you do that?"

Gremory took a seat on the desk. "Come here, Sebastian, let me tell you a secret."

He did, stopping just in front of her knees, as she brought her mouth to his ear. His breath hitched as she whispered.

"They all want somebody to believe in. They know what I am. The power I possess. So, they look to me for hope."

Sebastian pulled his ear away from her mouth to look her squarely in the eyes. "You're no mere lower-level demon, are you?"

Gremory giggled. "Oh no. In hell, I led over twenty-six legions. To some, I'd be deemed the closest thing this earth has seen to a god in a very, very long time."

Sebastian wasn't sure if he was dealing with fear or in awe of the being sitting before him.

The power and authority she possessed was terrifying. His question was as to why she was keeping him around.

Pulling him from his thoughts, she nudged his nose with hers and spoke directly into his lips. "What seems to be the problem, wolf?"

"Nothing," he lied.

"I love how resistant you are. There's something irresistible about the chase. And every time I kiss you, I love how the wolf in you fights to keep ahold of your soul. But that won't last long. Just wait until tonight."

Sebastian swallowed down the saliva that had made its way to his mouth. How a woman could be so terrifying and so seductive at once was beyond him.

He felt the urge to kiss her. He inched his lips closer to hers, barely a breath away and…

"Sebastian? Jennifer? What's…?" They turned to see Emerick behind them. "Oh no, Gremory!"

SEVENTEEN

Silence filled the Sheriff's Department as Deputy Olivia trailed in behind Emerick, who looked as if he hadn't slept in a week. Gremory got to her feet to approach him. "Emerick, I missed you. Don't be alarmed, I took the blame for those lost souls and now you're free."

"I thought we sent you to hell," he said through gritted teeth.

Gremory shrugged, in an almost childlike way, "What can I say? Your brother's love for me outweighed his desire for your plan."

"That lying son of a..."

"Oh, don't be mad. He had no knowledge of his actions. Just as you had no knowledge of what you were doing. You were the perfect vessel, Emerick. But your abstinence was such a nuisance. At least with that amulet you were asleep when I fed."

"How long until you set your eyes on Jennifer?"

"This stunning body? Only since the spell. That's right. Because of you, I was able to send an essence of myself into her. You should feel proud. We conquered a Morris witch together."

"You tricked me?"

"Of course, I did! That's what demons do, duh! Oh, but look at you. You look so drained. Let me fix that." On those words, she pulled his lips to her own, but he tried to pull away. "Oh, relax. You've been kissing me since Jennifer cast that first spell. You both have, you just didn't know it." On those words, Gremory turned to Sebastian who had brought his fingers to his mouth in surprise.

"Don't give me that look, wolf. Jennifer was there too. And she loved every minute of it. Why do you think she tried casting that unlove spell? No matter. Come! All of you. We have a party to be had. And I need to find the perfect dress. I think that girl, Chelsea, might have just what we need."

✳✳✳

After having dismissed Olivia to run a few errands in preparation for the Barrett Manor party, Gremory ordered Sebastian to drive the rest of them to Richmont High School. They found Chelsea at cheer practice alongside her cheer squad and the football team. "You're not on the cheers quad," Chelsea scoffed, mistaking Gremory for Jennifer, before turning her attention to Emerick. "But you're more than welcome to stay."

Deeply amused, Gremory brought her hand to girl's shoulder. "Do I look like Jennifer, you cunning little vixen?" While it might've sounded flirtatious to some, it wasn't received that way by Chelsea.

She jolted backwards and her entire demeanor dropped. "No... Who...? *What* are you?"

"Now, that's the respect I was looking for. I need you to fetch me a beautiful gown for tonight's party."

"What would you like?" Chelsea asked, simply submissive.

"You're a clever girl. Consider the dress you've always dreamed of wearing... Then that's the dress for me. Even if you have to beg, borrow or steal it. Do you understand?"

Fury and bitterness flooded through Chelsea, but she merely shook it away.

"Yes, right away." Chelsea fled, leaving Gremory the center of attention to the cheerleaders and the football team. And judging by the smile on her face, that's exactly what she wanted.

✳✳✳

By seven pm, the party at Barrett Manor was in full swing and it wasn't just the students from Richmont High who were in attendance, but anybody who was anybody, which included many visitors from out of town. As per Gremory's request, Emerick was made to play with Ambrose and the rest of the band. And as usual, their music was hypnotic to all who were present. Mortals and non-mortals alike.

The moment Gremory disappeared into one of the upstairs room, Sebastian, who was dressed in a neat grey collared shirt and black pants, searched for the rest of his team.

"Sebastian!" Marco Henderson called out, slapping his hand on Sebastian's back. "It feels like ages, dude! What's been going on?"

Sebastian stared at Marco awkwardly, before remembering Jennifer say something about Ambrose removing a groupie compulsion from him.

Clearly, the guy had no idea what had happened from the time Jennifer had kissed him and judging by Marco's overly rowdy demeanor, he was on the cusp of drunk. Evidently, the guys had brought their own alcohol to the event, which normally Sebastian would have reveled in. But this time, he pulled Marco away to speak in private. "Have you noticed anything weird about Jennifer lately?" he asked.

"Weird? About Jennifer? We're talking about your ex, right?"

"The one and only."

Marco's face scrunched up. "Well, there's also Daniella, word's out you two broke up? That true?"

While Daniella was still a tough topic, Sebastian needed to be straight with his friend. "Yeah, we did. How'd you find out?"

"She and Chelsea are telling everybody. So, if you're asking about Jennifer, clearly you two are looking to get back together. Is that the case?"

Marco clearly wasn't getting the point of Sebastian's conversation.

"Why do you ask?"

"Man, I've just always had a thing for Jennifer. And with she and I heading to the same college next year, I wanted to know if you'd have any objection if I were to..."

Sebastian's blood boiled. "Stay away from her, okay?"

"But you guys have been over for ages, what's the big deal?"

"Just drop it, alright? Besides, I need you and the guys to do something for me."

Marco's shoulders hunched, assuming his usual follower. "Alright, man. Whatever you need."

Hearing Marco speak of Jennifer in such a way was unsettling. Of course, they were supposed to go to the same college. Their families could only afford to send them to community college, while Sebastian had plans to go to a prestigious one in the city thanks to his football scholarship. For Marco to even think of dating her out of high school felt like a kick to the groin. Just then, Chelsea rushed over with a determined look across her face.

Sebastian and Chelsea had never really spoken throughout their entire school years. It was almost as if she were afraid of him. But it didn't bother him. In fact, he didn't trust her in the slightest.

"Sebastian, Jennifer needs you."

On her words, Sebastian tensed up, merely wishing that it was Jennifer that needed him and not that cunning demon.

"I'll go!" Marco said.

Sebastian turned to him. "Dude, no. I need you to stay here. Got that?"

Marco shrugged, before Sebastian turned back to Chelsea. "Give me a minute, okay? I need to chat with Marco first."

Chelsea took a step backwards while Sebastian whispered his plan into Marco's ear. After a look of confusion, Marco agreed, nonetheless.

Only a few minutes later, Chelsea led Sebastian up the stairs, and down the hallway in silence until Sebastian finally broke it. "You know what she is, don't you?"

She ignored him and kept walking. "Seriously, Chelsea. I know you know what's going on. Quit playing dumb."

That did it. Chelsea faced him.

For a moment she looked frightened, but she broke through that fear to oppose him. "Listen here, Sebastian Colby, what we're dealing with is far bigger than all of us. Of course, I know what she is. That's why I know the best thing for either of us to do is to shut up and obey. Or I promise you, it won't go down well."

"So, you're not enslaved to her?"

"Of course, I'm not. But I'm far more frightened of her, than I am of you. So, whatever you and Marco are planning, I'd drop it, because it's not worth it."

Without saying anything further, Chelsea raced on ahead until she reached a door on the right and knocked. After a brief moment, Chelsea opened it and led him into the room. The moment Sebastian laid eyes on Jennifer, he gasped. She was dressed in a slimming, strapless, red satin gown. Her hair was pulled back into a silver clip to accentuate the nape of her neck, with thin strands hanging over her face.

The blue amulet sat just above her cleavage, and she was wearing elegant black heels.

When she smiled at him, Sebastian forgot for the briefest of moments that he was staring at a demon and not the girl he had loved his whole life.

That was until she approached and said, "Chelsea, Sebastian. It feels so fitting that the three of you would be standing here with me. Chelsea knows what I'm talking about. Don't you?"

Sebastian gave Chelsea a confused look. But she merely kept her focus on Gremory.

After the piercing silence, Gremory continued. "Dear wolf, I'm assuming you're wondering why I summoned you here."

"It did cross my mind."

"Well, it just so happens that you're my date."

"Your date? Wouldn't it be more fitting to have Emerick accompany you? I mean, Jennifer was dating Emerick. If you wanted to keep up the perfect charade, it might've been more fitting to..."

"Emerick will be needed all in due time.

"For the ritual, right?"

"Yes, the ritual."

"So, what does it entail? Are you going to offer us as a blood sacrifice or something?"

"Oh no. Not blood. That's so messy. I want your souls. And I assure you, you'll love what I have planned."

"You're going to seduce us?"

Sebastian's very mind went right to Jennifer's vision. She had seen it all and it that moment, Sebastian knew he was done for.

"Is there a better way? How long have you waited to make love to Jennifer again? You'll certainly get your chance tonight."

"Nope. I'm not doing it. Not with you, and not with Emerick. So, stop toying with Jennifer and just let her go." Sebastian turned to leave so Gremory held her hand out to Chelsea. "The scissors, please, Chelsea."

"Yes, duchess," Chelsea took a pair from the dresser and handed them to Gremory, just as Sebastian turned back, curious as to what the demon had planned. Gremory held the scissors to her lower abdomen. "Jennifer is pregnant. It might not be your cub, but your soul will help this child grow so much stronger. If you refuse, I will stab these scissors into this body killing both Jennifer and her child. It's of no concern to me. I'm sure Chelsea would love to be the backup vessel."

Sebastian could never let that happen.

"Alright fine!" He returned to Gremory's side and linked his right arm through hers. Gremory linked her right arm through Chelsea's and the three of them left the room.

With Jennifer and her baby's life on the line, Sebastian vowed to himself that he would do whatever he could to save Jennifer no matter what it took. Jennifer could hate him later.

✳ ✳ ✳

Having a demon controlling her body was torture. Jennifer couldn't speak the words she wanted to speak.

Nor could she move her body in the way she wanted to. All she could do was just sit and watch as Gremory piloted her every action, as if she were paralyzed.

Gremory had already proven numerous times that she could read her thoughts just by sheer will, so Jennifer was stumped at how to beat the demon at her own game.

However, thanks to the ability the demon held to plug into her thoughts, Jennifer had been made privy to Gremory's plans.

The hell duchess planned on seducing Sebastian and Emerick during the ritual, which would end in her devouring both their souls.

The souls of an incubus and a cursed lover would not only strengthen Gremory's powers, but also eliminate their chances of stopping her.

The souls of the party guests were the next on the menu. The more souls Gremory devoured, the stronger she would become and eventually Richmont would be wiped off the map.

While those fears had Jennifer strategizing a way out of her predicament, it was Gremory's plans for Jennifer's unborn child that chilled her very core.

Jennifer's child would be born of an incubus and a Morris Witch. Adding in the fact that Jennifer was the child of an angel would really make her offspring a rare miracle. From the backseat in Jennifer's mind, she watched as Sebastian and Chelsea led her down the corridor towards the staircase. According to Gremory, it was because of their supposed ties, that they were immune to the demon's lure. That very notion baffled Jennifer as she had studied the story of Rose Morris extensively and Chelsea Lee's name had never been mentioned anywhere in the spell book.

However, their supposed immunity meant that Jennifer's only hope of breaking free of Gremory relied on them.

She could hear that hypnotic music playing, only emphasizing that the party was in full swing.

As they reached the top of the stairs, the music stopped. Lulled into a calm silence, the audience looked to Ambrose to address them. Which he did, proudly. "Ladies and gentlemen, welcome to Barrett Manor. Let me introduce our beautiful host, the mistress with the most, Jennifer Morris."

While the applause was flattering, Jennifer only wished she was able to enjoy it. Instead, she could feel Gremory loving every minute. And it was that enjoyment which gave Jennifer an idea. With the demon distracted by her own narcissism, she used every ounce of her powers to get a message to Sebastian. "Colby, you need to get out of here."

He turned to her. "Jennifer? I'm leaving you. How can you even think that?"

Before Jennifer could respond, Gremory scolded her inside her very mind. '*Good try, witch. But not good enough.*'

But Jennifer had already succeeded once, which meant that it was possible to try again. She just needed the perfect distraction.

As the applause died down, Sebastian and Chelsea led Gremory to the stage, where Emerick set down his guitar and escorted her to the microphone. Jennifer could've sworn she saw Sebastian and Emerick send one another a look but couldn't tell if it was just animosity between the two or not. Gremory took the microphone and addressed the crowd delivering the message that Jennifer dreaded to hear. "Mortals, non-mortals, and demons alike. Yes mortals, you heard that right. You live in a world where you have been forced to live side-by-side with the monsters you thought only existed in your nightmares. But whether you are afraid of one another or not doesn't matter. The doors have already been locked so you cannot escape. Nor why would you with such beautiful music?" She paused to stroke Ambrose's cheek playfully before turning back to the audience.

"For so long we have had to keep to the shadows, but tonight, I say no more. Let us no longer be afraid to show our true faces. Let us dance, drink, and be merry for tomorrow we shall see a new dawn!"

Once Gremory finished her speech, there was a roar of applause as Ambrose led the band into a new song. One with a slow-paced rhythm, but was lacking with a lead guitar, for Emerick had left the stage. As if on cue, members of the audience began to change shape. Humans turned into wolves. Shredded wings broke out of the backs of disguised sirens. But nobody seemed to notice.

As Gremory left the stage to join her dates, Sebastian was the first to argue his point. "How could you? We're supposed to be keeping our identities a secret!"

"They've been living in the shadows for so long," Gremory said. "But not anymore. It's time to live freely. Chelsea, would you mind bringing Emerick up to the ritual room in half an hour. Keep him entertained until then."

"Yes, duchess." Chelsea followed after Emerick, who was making his way through the crowd, leaving Gremory alone with Sebastian.

"That music really is beautiful. Too bad we can't dance to it. I'm eager to get our little party started." She pulled Sebastian back towards the stairwell, until they were stopped by a furious Daniella. "Sebastian, Jennifer? How could you? We only just broke up. I'm carrying your child!"

Sebastian went to voice his apology, until Gremory cut him off. "Daniella, please don't be mad. You must understand that I simply need Sebastian. You see, with his soul I'll be able to perform a ritual that will bring about a new beginning for your child and mine. Is that okay?"

Daniella stood no chance. She caved to the demon's thrall. "I'm so sorry. It won't happen again. May I kiss your feet in forgiveness?"

"That won't be necessary. Just leave."

Daniella nodded and left them in peace. But Sebastian was furious. He shoved Gremory, in anger and she didn't even flinch. "How could you? You leave Daniella out of this. She's innocent!"

"I never thought you'd lay a hand on a pregnant woman, Sebastian. What's the matter? Is your testosterone flaring? I imagine it would be considering you would be feeling the urge to shift into a wolf, right about now. But I have simply paused your transition... Until we complete the ritual that is."

"I won't take part in your stupid ritual! You can't make me!" Even though Jennifer respected Sebastian's disobedience, there was a part of her that wished he would stop putting himself in harm's way, for he seemed to be the demon's favorite toy. Gremory resorted to using the Morris Charm on him, and in doing so, made it impossible for Jennifer to access that ability.

Gremory ran Sebastian's hands up her sides then whispered with sweet seduction.

"Let's go, Sebastian. Let's start the ritual." While those words made Jennifer wish she had never cast that spell, it was Sebastian's mindless response that would change things between them forever.

"Yes, duchess. I'm at your service.

EIGHTEEN

Gremory led Sebastian into a room that was fit for a queen and just like most of the furniture at Barrett Manor, the large bed was draped in burgundy satin while the frame was made of mahogany. An armchair sat by the window and a large chest of drawers sat at the far end of the room. A royal red rug with a golden pentagram crafted into it spread across the varnished flooring and a golden chandelier hung from the ceiling above. Entranced, Sebastian guided her to the bed, by the hand, while Jennifer fought hard against the demon's resistance.

At the bed, Sebastian cupped her chin in his hand and with every action he made Jennifer could see him trying to break free. "Morris... if you're in there... I don't want to... arghh.... Do anything you're not comfortable with."

Jennifer tried to do the same.

She tried.

And struggled...

Then finally she managed to release Sebastian's hand and pull away.

"Stupid girl!" Gremory snapped out loud. "I could kill you, right now. I am far stronger than you could ever be. Downstairs, there is an entire crowd worshipping me, fueling my power." With a stretch of her neck, Gremory had full control of Jennifer again and with that control, she kissed Sebastian.

With just a kiss, Sebastian was hers again. He wrapped his arms around her, brought his hands to the back of her dress, and slowly unzipped it.

'Come on, Sebastian, fight it!' Jennifer cried out within her mind. But as his lips found her neck, she

knew she only wanted him to keep going. It was selfish to want him so much. She would've loved to blame that desire entirely on Gremory, but knew she couldn't. For she loved Sebastian more than she should have. More than the Morris-Colby curse should allow.

Gremory tore Sebastian's shirt open, snapping every single button along the way and moved her hands to remove his pants. Her lips crashed against his chest. He moaned, which only frustrated Jennifer more.

How dare he enjoy it?

He should've been fighting her away.

Jennifer's dress slipped to the floor, leaving her standing in nothing more than her purple lace underwear. She pulled down his pants to reveal his black briefs and her mind flooded back to their first time. While most people would complain that their first times didn't go so well, Sebastian had ensured theirs had gone perfectly. He had organized a picnic under the stars and even snuck his parents' expensive wine which tasted horrible.

Now, they were in the perfect position to relive that experience and her head seemed to blur at all the reasons why they shouldn't.

She didn't want to fight it and she could tell that neither did he. Sebastian returned his lips to hers, lifted her up in his arms, so that her legs wrapped around his waist, and laid her on the bed. He took a moment to catch his breath and as he did, Jennifer managed to take ahold of herself.

"Sebastian," she gasped.

"Jennifer. I'm trying to stop myself." But Jennifer didn't want him to stop.

Instead, she pulled his head to hers, as he positioned his body over hers. He ran his hand up the back of her thigh, trailed his kiss from her neck to her breast and continued downwards until his face was between her legs.

Temporarily free from Gremory's compulsion, Jennifer first tried to determine why the demon had stepped aside in her mind. Her second thought was of how Sebastian had certainly improved his technique since the last time they had been together. And her third thought was how the hell were they going to trap that damn demon?

Emerick led Chelsea to the closed main entrance of Barrett Manor. Earlier that night Sebastian had devised a plan to free as many of the guests as possible. Unfortunately, while Gremory saw Sebastian as her own personal lapdog, it meant that Emerick needed to carry out the full weight of the plan. The very thought of Gremory's compulsion over them aggravated him, but he was too much of a liability. He tried to open the door and just as he had thought, it was locked.

Sebastian had already persuaded some of the football players and cheerleaders to take their friends and leave before the doors had been sealed. But the hall was still far from empty.

There were so many mortals and non-mortals that he didn't recognize and so many bodies of the dead being piloted by demons. Emerick was certain that many of those demons had come from the amulet. All around him vampires, sirens, and other non-mortals feasted hungrily on mortals as if they had never feasted before and nobody did a thing to stop it. Just like an incubi's prey felt nothing but pleasure until the moment they died. He understood the similarity, but still he hated it.

Jennifer had been a simple distraction from how much he hated that damn curse. His goal had been to find the killer, stop them and leave. But of course, Gremory had other plans.

Despite how hard Emerick tried to fight her, she would always have that leash on them. But while he hated her with a vengeance, Ambrose would always be nothing more than a toy soldier to the hell duchess, leaving Emerick to pick up the pieces.

"She wants us to join them," Chelsea said. Her voice, like nails on a chalkboard. Emerick raced over to the opened window.

Outside, he could see a crowd gathering... Leading the crowd was Marian Morris. They wouldn't be able to get in. He tried to punch his fist through the window. It had been sealed with hellfire, making it impenetrable.

"Emerick," Chelsea continued. "You shouldn't keep her waiting."

That was it. Emerick turned to her with the sheer temptation to snap her neck.

"The last thing we should be doing is going up there. Do you even know what she has planned?"

Chelsea retreated, but only slightly. "Of course, I do. It's a sex ritual."

"Stop thinking like a whore! That ritual will kill everybody who is present here tonight, including you, Sebastian and maybe even Jennifer."

"I don't know about that. Well, Sebastian, yes. But Gremory and I have an understanding. If we lose Jennifer, she'll use me as the next vessel. Besides, look at you. You're looking exhausted. Pale even." She stepped closer so there was barely an inch of distance between them. He was exhausted. Drained of energy. He hadn't devoured a soul in so damn long and was growing tired of Chelsea's screeching voice. "When was the last time you had the slightest taste of a soul. You need this just as much as I do, Emerick." She ran her hands up his torso leaving him struggling to fight an exhaustive battle. The girl bore no charm over him. But he was hungry and growing desperate. His lips hovered towards hers. Desperate to feed, but also trying to resist. But then he saw a figure standing in his peripheral vision. She should've been dead. Emerick turned to see Aisha standing before them. Beside her was another girl he recognized. Her name was Cassandra Blake.

She had been a friend of his and the first death that had taken place in Richmont since the killings had begun. The blond girl behind them he assumed was Emma Bryce. All lives he had taken. But of course, they were nothing more than shell cases for demons to pilot. That must've been Gremory's plan all along. She wasn't killing the mortals but using them for her legion of demons.

"Emerick, it's been so long," Piress, the demon possessing Aisha, said. Chelsea gasped, as if she knew exactly what she was in the presence of.

Piress had been a general in one of the legions of hell. She sought pleasure in torturing her victims. She had even tortured Emeric for a few centuries.

"Piress," Emerick nodded. "Leave these people alone. They're not worth your time."

"I beg to differ. Now, excuse me. I'm a little thirsty." Piress bore her fangs and then raised her hand. Her powers sent Emerick flying backwards into the crowd before she ripped into the neck of a nearby mortal. With demons like Piress around and the doors locked, Emerick needed to do something fast. Even if it meant going up stairs to disrupt Gremory's personal party with Sebastian.

✳ ✳ ✳

It took a lot to scare Marian Morris, but as she peered up at the old mansion that was Barrett Manor, she was met by the gut-wrenching terror that haunted her memories. Fifteen years had passed since she had last tread on that cursed soil.

She could've easily have gone another fifteen years, but again, fate had others plans. At least she wasn't alone. Standing a short distance away was Sheriff Mike ready and waiting for her to give the order.

He and Marian had been out to lunch when Gremory had taken over the will of the Deputy and it was only thanks to the surveillance footage that they had any idea what had occurred at all.

Standing with Marian was her coven. Sure, they weren't real witches. They were mortals. But it was their belief in the craft that strengthened Marian's powers. And right now, she needed that.

Knowing that they were dealing with the hypnotic music of an incubi, Marian had cast a tone-deaf hearing spell on her coven to prevent them from hearing the beauty of the music.

"This won't go well," Cindy Burrows, Marian's best friend, and Jennifer's school principal said, from beside her.

"My reading foretold that many will die, tonight."

She might've been a mere mortal, but her knack for reading tarot cards impressed even Marian herself.

"More will die if we stand around and do nothing, Cindy. But if it's any consolation Sebastian succeeded in getting some of them to leave earlier."

"I just wish I knew what we were dealing with when Jennifer first came to the clinic," Violet said. "We could've intervened earlier. But I thought it was a simple love spell. Not…"

"…No point living in regret, Violet," Marian replied. "We're dealing with it now."

Just as Marian spoke those words, they were joined by a large group of men. Leading the pack, was somebody Marian would've preferred to steer clear of… Fernando Colby.

He was merely an older, grumpier version of his son, Sebastian, and as he approached Marian, he spoke in a gruff voice, with his dark eyes focused entirely on the large manor. "Fifteen years. I thought we were done with this place and done with being pulled into the Morris-Colby curse nonsense."

"Hello to you too, Fernando. You're looking a little greyer around the ears these days." She sniffed him. "And you smell like a dog that fell into a barrel of his owner's whiskey."

He turned to her. Angry. "My son is in there. Why aren't we?"

"Quit your whining. They've sealed the windows and doors using hellfire. My magic can't break through. Besides, that *thing* has both our children captive. So, the least we can do is create a spell so strong to break down that barrier."

Fernando narrowed his eyes. He knew what she was planning, and he was thoroughly against it.

"You want to channel our connection again. Don't you?"

"It worked last time, and it'll work this time too."

Fernando shook his head, raised his shoulders, and opposed her with the authority of a true alpha. "For Christ's sake, Marian. We should've burned this goddam place down when we sealed that pit shut. If it wasn't for you and your goddamn daughter, Sebastian wouldn't..."

But Marian would not take his insults lying down like his pack would. She clenched her fist shut in front of him, forcing his mouth to close, then brought her face mere inches from his. The fury in her eyes and the power she held over him was evident to all those present.

"...Listen, Fernando. Don't you ever talk about my daughter that way again. I want this connection broken just as much as you do. Burning this place down would've done nothing because it's this land the demons are attracted to. And I get that you're not a fan of the Morris-Colby curse, neither am I. But like it or not, we can't stop it. So, we can either fight it out right here or you can let me use that connection to break down that wall... and I promise, if you choose the latter, we can and *will* go back to hating one another after."

Marian opened her hand, immediately allowing Fernando to take a breath. "Now, what do you say?"

Fernando looked around, embarrassed, but he lowered his guard, nonetheless.

"Just make sure you keep that promise, witch."

"Won't be hard. You've never been a very likeable man."

Fernando ignored her final comment as he turned to his men, who were waiting for his orders, and he gave his command as one might lead an army. Admirably.

"Wolves! We do as the witch orders. If she needs blood. We bleed!"

✳✳✳

Fighting for self-control against a demon was by far, the hardest thing Jennifer had ever had to do. But that battle was made even more difficult thanks to the way Sebastian was kissing her thighs.

Fortunately, with Gremory's full focus on summoning forth the souls from the floor below, the demon had left Jennifer's thoughts alone.

In turn, Jennifer was left to strategize amidst her battle of composure against the distraction that was Sebastian Colby. Thanks to the telepathic communication link she shared with her mother, she was aware that Marian had gathered an army consisting of her coven and the town's wolves.

That very army was gathered right outside channeling the Morris-Colby Curse.

Unfortunately, channeling the Morris-Colby curse was exactly what Gremory was doing to strengthen her ritual. It was the perfect source of power and the very reason Gremory had chosen to seduce Sebastian first. But it was Jennifer's belief in her abilities that fueled her craft.

The very thought of having an untapped mental connection brought Jennifer's mind back to Sebastian. Just maybe, their mental connection was the answer to breaking his compulsion.

Because, despite how good he made her feel, he would surely die if she didn't try to save him.

Just as Jennifer used all her willpower to open a telepathic link, Gremory grabbed Sebastian's head and pulled him to her mouth. Jennifer was met by her own want, need, and hunger for him.

And as his hand traced her thigh, she willed herself to scream out to him in her mind.

'Colby, stop!"

His eyes flickered open. She was certain that he had heard her. *'Morris, I swear to you, I'm trying to stop. But Gremory... she's using that damn lure.'*

He was right. Gremory was strong. But they needed to be stronger.

'I know it's like our bodies have a mind of their own, but if we don't stop, Gremory will devour your soul.'

'You think I don't know that? But I just can't control myself. She's banking on the fact that I would literally die for you.'

He was right. If it wasn't for the curse, Sebastian wouldn't be compelled to Jennifer in a way that would force him to offer up his own life.

It was the ultimate act of worship, and he had no choice but to submit. And consequently, Jennifer was just along for the ride. But as her body welcomed him willingly, she tried to consider the best course of action.

It was Sebastian's next thought that merely escalated their problem.

'*I know this is the worst time to bring this up because we're literally about to do it, but do you remember when I said, sometimes I can't help how hormones impact...?*'

'*...Just spit it out, Colby.*'

'*Lobo kinda wants out.*'

Jennifer wanted to laugh at how he had phrased that problem. Was he referring to the appendage between his legs as *Lobo* or...?

Wait...

No, Lobo was the soul of his wolf.

And while Sebastian's entire body was rigidly battling his physical urges, Jennifer could see the dark fur growing at his neck. The amber in his eyes dominating the dark brown.

'*Seriously? Now?*' she scoffed.

'Sorry. It's just too hard. If I keep fighting Gremory, Lobo will take over in a bid to protect me and I'm not strong enough to fight them both. But if I don't fight it...'

'...I get it.'

They had no choice. Sebastian had to stop fighting his urges for her. He either had to give into Gremory or Lobo. Just as she entertained the thought it dawned on her. Just maybe she could use Sebastian's soul as bait. Which, in turn, could give her the opportunity to recite a banishing spell.

It was her only shot.

'Alright, Colby. Then that's what we'll do. Stop fighting it. Give in to your urges and let me do the rest. Okay?

He looked at her, utterly confused but still fighting his inner battles and with nothing else left to lose, his hesitant response came.

'*Okay, but I hope you know what you're doing.*' He wasn't the only one who was holding onto that hope. She was clinging to it with every ounce of desperation.

Sebastian was perfect. His very movements alone were enough to send her senses into hyperdrive. But despite her overpowering urge to lose herself, she needed to keep a level head.

Then came the moment that Sebastian pulled his mouth from hers. The amber in his eyes had been replaced by his fearful brown. That fear surged as his transparent white soul poured from his lips towards hers. Gremory's hunger for it was overpowering.

As Sebastian's musky scent passed her lips and travelled into her body, Jennifer fought for her own self-control and forced the words to pour from her lips. "Summoning forth the…"

As she spoke, Gremory took control of her words. "Shut up, witch!"

So, Jennifer struggled harder.

"Argh! No, Summoning, forth the magic from the Morris-Colby curse, I, Jennifer Morris banish you…"

Before she could finish, the door to the room flung open and crashed onto the floor. Emerick had broken it down in a bid to save her.

Gremory took back Jennifer's sense of control and turned to Emerick.

"Oh, Emerick. It's about time you joined the party. I've exhausted the soul of Sebastian."

To Jennifer's horror, Gremory pushed Sebastian's unconscious body to the side and climbed out of the bed.

Jennifer's plan had failed and now she couldn't even check to see if he was okay. She knew that she had consumed too much of him for the outcome to be remotely good.

Gremory made her way to Emerick with the sheer desire to seduce him, but Emerick met her with full opposition. "Get out of her head, Gremory!" he ordered.

"Why the hostility? Are you forgetting who you're talking to?"

She brought her hands to his throat and her lips to his mouth, threatening to squeeze the very essence from him.

"You are nothing but cannon fodder in my army. The only reason you possess such a gift is because I made it so. Don't you remember those early days in hell? Those days where I pulled you from the hands of Piress as she whipped you and your brother mercilessly? I gave you a purpose and I can just as easily take it from you."

As Emerick struggled to speak, a black smoke emerged from his mouth. His eyes turned black, remaining fixed on the amulet at Jennifer's neck.

"Je...Jennifer. I... I know you're in there. You and Sebastian... you... you need to fight it. For our child."

"It's not going to work, lover boy," Gremory smirked, turning her head back to the bed, where a large black wolf with amber eyes was now standing with its back arched ready to strike.

"Hey Lobo," Gremory said with a sinister smile. "Dinner is served."

On those words, the demon threw the body of Emerick to the floor and the large black wolf made its attack. With a combination of blood, bites, and vicious blows, Emerick fought Lobo as a demon might fight off a wild animal.

Jennifer was horrified. Clearly, with the essence of Sebastian, Gremory held the power to control Lobo. Which was a shock because even Sebastian struggled with that order.

She wondered if Gremory was intending on letting Lobo kill Emerick, or if it was merely to weaken him into submission.

Either case wasn't good. But as she watched the very wounded Emerick hold Lobo's mouth shut, while pushing his entire weight into him, she couldn't help but hear the words he called out.

"Jennifer, listen to me. Aisha's soul is in that amulet. Her body has been taken over by a demon. Just like yours. You need to fight it. For the sake of our child. You're a Morris witch. You have the…"

Gremory knocked Emerick off the wolf. "Jennifer is no more," she snarled. As the wolf readied his next attack, Emerick spoke with such wounded conviction.

"I know you're in there Jennifer. Lobo might be the wolf that resides in Sebastian. But he's your familiar. His soul obeys you. Only you can stop

Gremory, so do it for our daughter. Do it for Sebastian. Please."

Those were the words that could destroy a legion of demons and they fueled Jennifer's very core. And they made a hell of a lot of sense.

Lobo was attacking Emerick because Gremory was controlling her will. Jennifer summoned forth the magic of herself. The magic of her unborn child... and the soul of Sebastian which was still coursing through her veins to banish Gremory from her body. "I summon forth the magic from the Morris-Colby curse. I summon forth all the power from every Morris Witch living or dead... I summon forth the magic of my own child. A child born of Morris blood and incubi. I summon forth the soul of Sebastian Colby to banish you out of my body, Gremory! Now get the hell out!"

Jennifer's body convulsed, and her mouth spewed forth a black smokey essence which lifted into the air and floated towards the roof, choosing to circle the chandelier. She removed the amulet from her neck and held it up towards the eerie black soul. "By the power of the Morris-Colby curse, I order you, Gremory, to enter this am..."

"...You have no authority over me, girl!" an eerie hag-like voice snarled from the smoke.

"I would like to thank you for the essence of a cursed lover. It's the perfect sacrifice to carry out my plans."

Before Jennifer could comprehend what had happened, the black smoke disappeared into the pentagram rug, leaving Emerick to assist Jennifer back into the gown. After he had zipped up the back of the dress for her. "She's taken Sebastian," Jennifer said, that it was the gut-wrenching truth.

"I know."

"She will not get away with this!"

NINETEEN

There was a bloodbath in the great hall and while the music magically played, Ambrose was no longer on the stage. He had just finished sucking the souls of his own band members. The screams of mortals could be heard for miles as they became the feasts of demons and the hypnotized non-mortals.

Above the chaos, white souls of the dead floated up towards the roof and encircled a large black cloud that had emerged from the room above.

Amongst the crowd, an eight-tailed fox scurried about until it found a dark-haired girl of about seventeen years of age curled up under a table, traumatized... *Daniella.*

The fox sat beside her, then transformed into the one and only... "Chelsea? How did...? What...?"

"No time to explain. I know you're scared, but we need to get out of here."

"We can't. The doors are locked. Jennifer... she and Sebastian..."

While Chelsea would've loved to dive into the honestly exhausting train-wreck that was the Morris-Colby curse, she had more important things to worry about. Like making sure Daniella's unborn child survived. Chelsea's very existence depended on it. "Just, shut up for one minute, okay? The last thing I need to hear is about that witch. Let's just get to safety. There are rooms up the stairs and down the hall. If we stay down here our souls will be transported up through the roof and we will die. Do you understand?"

Daniella considered the question, then looked around at the chaos beyond the table. She was utterly terrified. "What if they catch us?"

"Just leave that to me but when I say 'go', we go. Okay?"

Daniella stifled an unsure nod, so Chelsea placed her hand on her. The moment she did, they both became invisible. "Okay, let's go!" Chelsea said, taking her hand. Reluctantly, Daniella followed Chelsea up the stairs and down the corridor, passing Jennifer, Emerick, and Lobo, who were entirely oblivious to them, along the way.

✳ ✳ ✳

Side-by-side the twenty-seven witches of Marian's coven and the thirty-two wolves of Fernando's pack encircled Barrett Manor hand-in-hand chanting the words, "*Fortioresd Una. Nos*

Advocabit Uriel. Fortioresd Una. Nos Advocabit Uriel. Fortioresd Una. Nos Advocabit Uriel."

In unison, the voices shifted the energy of the night invoking a large gust of wind to engulf the building before them.

"It doesn't seem to be working." Fernando said to Marian.

"Believe me. It's working," Marian snapped back. "Now just keep chanting like your son's life depends on it!"

Fernando obeyed and continued to chant the words over, and over. The winds grew stronger and stronger, threatening to sweep them into the cyclone too. Thunder echoed all around summoning forth a large and almighty storm. Hard rain threatened to flash flood, but the support the witches and wolves offered one another kept them grounded. Then came the moment Marian had been waiting for. She turned to Fernando and smiled. "You might want to shut your eyes, old friend."

Before he could, a blinding light lit up the center of the cyclone. It grew in shape and luminosity until it exploded, illuminating the night.

"That's our cue," Marian shouted. "The door seals have been broken. I'm sure you remember the scent of a demon, Fernando?"

"Don't remind me."

"Good, because now's our chance to bust in there and rip them all to shreds. Bring out Duke."

With an irritated roll of the eyes and an incoherent grunt, Fernando raised his hand, signaling the order to the rest of his pack.

Then, in a frightening display of power, starting with Fernando, the bodies of the men, grew fur, contorted, and transformed into ravenous wolves.

Delighted, Marian patted the large black and grey wolf which had taken Fernando's form, on the head. "Make me proud, Duke," she said. "Go get them!" On her order, the wolf, known as Duke, took off into Barrett Manor leading the rest of the wolves into the thick of war.

❋ ❋ ❋

As Jennifer stormed the corridor, flexing her wrists, and considering the thought that she might never see Sebastian again, she felt the presence of an invisible force pass by. But her current vengeance would be taken out on the mass of black smoke that circled the chandelier "That bitch dies tonight!" Jennifer said.

"Don't do this!" Ambrose's voice carried out from behind she, Emerick and Lobo, forcing them to turn around. Lobo cut into the space in front of Jennifer, growling at Ambrose.

"Stand down, Ambrose," Emerick warned. "We're bringing her down once and for all."

"After everything Gremory has done for us, how could you be so ungrateful?"

"Are you forgetting the endless list of people she's killed?" Jennifer broke in. "All those cases you were so determined to solve?"

"That was until I learned the truth. You see, Jennifer, Aisha isn't dead. None of them are. Their souls are tucked safe and sound in that amulet at your neck." Jennifer thumbed the amulet, then glanced down at the chaos in the hall.

It was filled with demons and non-mortals feasting on the innocents. People she had seen and lived side-by-side with and so many others. It broke her heart. And amongst the demons was Aisha. No, not Aisha. Just her body being used as a vessel.

Suddenly, the windows and doors were smashed in from the outside and large wolves tore into the building fighting off demons and feral non-mortals alike. They were followed in by the witches from Marian's coven who were chanting in unison.

In the middle of the battle, Jennifer saw Aisha using what could've only been explained as superspeed to snap necks and unleash the souls from each body.

The sight made Jennifer sick to her stomach. She turned back to Ambrose.

"That's not Aisha."

"No, that's a demon, sweetie," Ambrose said casually. "And there's so many down there, you stand no chance of fighting them all."

"Maybe not," Emerick said, his voice filled with exhaustion. "But we'll die trying. Even if it means taking you down with us."

Jennifer took in Emerick's façade and could tell that he hadn't feasted in a while. She, having had more than enough energy, removed the amulet.

"What are you doing?" he asked her.

"Take the amulet. If Ambrose doesn't stand down, we'll need to suck his soul into it."

She handed him the amulet, and with it, a ball of energy to ensure he wouldn't die of exhaustion. It wouldn't be as good as a soul, but it would hopefully do the trick.

"And how do we trap his soul without Gremory?" Emerick asked.

"I've laced the amulet with a spell. If Ambrose dies, he'll be trapped. Now you deal with him. I'll deal with the hell duchess."

Without giving him the chance to argue, Jennifer raced halfway down the stairs until she was surrounded in a blend of thick black, red, and white smoke. *The souls.*

She focused on the memory of Sebastian. He was dead for having trusted her.

She focused on channeling the powers of the Morris-Colby curse, of every Morris witch that ever existed... And of her unborn child.

She focused on whatever angel essence of her father that she had and looked to her mother, who was telepathically keeping the demons away from her. With all the energy possessed, Jennifer screamed the words at the top of her lungs. "In the name of the goddess, Hekate, I banish thee, Gremory beyond the realms of the living. In the name of every Morris witch ever to exist. In the name of the angels. In the name of vengeance, I banish thee straight back to hell, you soul sucking bitch!" The black billowing smoke trailed towards her at incredible speed, speaking with that same sinister voice that had taken Sebastian's soul.

"Sure, I'll go to hell. But I'm taking you and your child along with me."

"Get down!" Emerick cried out, but he was too far away. Instead, Jennifer was slammed to the ground by Lobo. Her head smacked against the wooden step, and the weight of the beast almost concealed her view. But Jennifer needed to see. Needed to be sure the spell worked.

She peered out from under the wolf to see the black smoke of Gremory explode into the floor right beside them. A bright light illuminated the space where the black smoke had disappeared.

As if a light as bright as the sun had been flicked on in the hall, the entire room lit up, forcing many to shield their eyes. When it had finally dulled again, the black smoke was gone.

Gremory was gone.

But while Lobo was still with her, where was Sebastian? And where the hell had the light come from?

But Jennifer had no time for contemplations. She needed to find Aisha. And so, with Lobo on her tail, she disappeared into the chaos still unfolding around her.

✳✳✳

With Jennifer having disappeared into the crowd, Emerick stood opposing Ambrose.

"I never thought I'd see the day you'd turn your back on your own kind, brother," Ambrose said. "You know she can't give you a normal life, so why try?"

"She's pregnant with my child, Ambrose. It doesn't get any more normal than that."

Surprise hit Ambrose like a ton of bricks. But it was accompanied by a mixture of other emotions too. "But that's not..."

"...It's the truth. So, help me find a way to live side by side with the non-mortals and mortals in a way that doesn't require us to make groupies or devour the souls of the innocent."

"Gremory was a god and you sent her back to hell. There's no hope for any of us. Least of all that child of yours."

"You're wrong."

"Am I? Well, I guess we'll see then, shall we?" Picking up on his brother's empty tone, Emerick knew his brother was planning something.

He peered down at the shard of glass in the man's hand, which had come from one of the smashed windows. Ambrose had loved Gremory as a lover, a leader, and a god. Being forced to live an eternity apart from Gremory was sure to be the worst torment.

"Don't do it, Ambrose. Don't..." Emerick said.

Ambrose tightened his grip around the glass. Black blood seeped onto the red rug and in the time it took Emerick to reach his brother, Ambrose had already slit his own throat. His red soul flooded into the amulet at Emerick's neck. Emerick didn't move.

Sure, his brother wasn't dead. They were demons. Immortal life was a guarantee. Though deep down, he knew Ambrose was right.

Emerick would never have the chance at a normal life. And neither would his child.

✳ ✳ ✳

Alongside Lobo, Jennifer rushed through the crowd in search of Aisha's vessel, when at last, she saw her feasting on a mortal man.

Her eyes were black, and her face was caked in blood. She looked horrifying.

Jennifer thought back to the white light that had appeared when she had banished Gremory and wondered if it had something to do with her angel lineage. It made sense because normally her Morris Witch powers had no effect on demons.

With that thought in mind, she wondered if there was a way to use that angel light to put Aisha's soul back into her body.

"Unhand my friend's body!" Jennifer yelled, running over to Piress, who turned to her in sheer amazement.

"Your friend? I was wondering where Gremory acquired this exquisite little thing."

"Give her back!"

The grin on Aisha's face deepened. "Or what, Witch? You'll sic your dog on me? Have you any idea who…"

"Lobo, now!"

On Jennifer's command, the wolf pounced on Aisha, distracting her as Jennifer looked to Emerick who was rushing towards them. "Emerick, the amulet!"

In the time it took him to race over, Jennifer had already transported the amulet from his neck to her hand. "Okay, get back, Lobo." Again, Lobo obeyed.

He retreated just in time for Jennifer to hold up the stone and begin to chant.

"I summon forth all angel essence within my being to banish the demons from the bodies of the innocents. *Animus reparo, animus substituo. Animus reparo, animus substituo.*"

In seconds, the amulet lifted into the air and all the souls around them encircled the stone before entering it, including the demon souls that possessed Aisha and Emma Bryce. At the same time, some of the souls that had been in the amulet, poured out in search of their original bodies.

Black, red, and white smoke spread amongst the crowds who were either injured or remorseful of what they had done. It would take more than just Marian's herbal teas to wipe those memories away.

When the smokey essences had all disappeared, Jennifer took in the sight of the wounded.

The chaos was no more.

Before her, Aisha sat covered in bloodied wounds and utterly terrified. "Jen… Jennifer?"

"Oh, Aisha. I'm so sorry." Jennifer swooped Aisha into her arms and hugged her, taking note of her bloodied wounds.

"Oww!" Aisha groaned.

"It's okay, let me fix them. I can heal…" Jennifer said, resting her hand on her friend's shoulder.

"…What are you doing?!"

"Don't be scared. I'm just trying to help."

The moment Jennifer spoke those words, Aisha's wounds began to mend.

But the look of horror in Aisha's eyes was permanent as they drifted to Emerick.

"Jennifer, you need to get away from him! He's a monster."

"I'm sorry," Emerick began.

"It's okay," Jennifer tried to assure her. "That wasn't Emerick. He was possessed."

"Possessed? What...? What do you mean, possessed?" As Jennifer tried to figure out how to give the apology that Aisha clearly wasn't ready to hear, Marian approached and placed her hand on Aisha's shoulder. "Hello, Aisha. It's been a while. Right now, you need to forget what you've seen here and go home to bed. Okay? Jennifer will bring you some tea tomorrow and your parents... Well, I will come and visit them later."

Aisha blinked and in seconds she was compelled to forget. She left the house in a trance.

Marian, on the other hand, turned back to Jennifer. "We have a problem, Jennifer."

As Lobo nuzzled into Jennifer's side, she noticed the grief in Fernando Colby's eyes.

It brought the sheer weight of what that problem was straight to the forefront of her mind. Sebastian's soul was in hell.

TWENTY

Sebastian's funeral was held three days later, and during those days, Marian worked to provide the town with an herbal tea that was designed to help them deal with the trauma of all they had seen the night of Gremory's party. But Jennifer refused to take the tea. She refused to take anything that would force her to forget Sebastian.

His service was held under dark clouds that promised rain and there was a chill in the air.

To Jennifer, the miserable weather went perfectly with her mood. While nobody would admit it to her face, she knew that he had gone to hell because of her. He had trusted her, and she had betrayed that trust. She should've been stronger than Gremory. She should've…

Mid-thought, Jennifer saw Aisha watching her from the mourning crowd. The service was over, and the friends and family of Sebastian were speaking quietly amongst themselves.

Jennifer had just finished speaking with Sebastian's mother, Anamaria, who had done her best to keep her chin held high. Jennifer had always adored the woman and according to Sebastian those feelings had always been mutual.

As Jennifer gave the short darkhaired woman another long hug, she excused herself to speak with Aisha, who had arrived with her older brother, Joey.

"I'm leaving Richmont," Aisha said once Jennifer had joined her.

"What do you mean?"

But Aisha refused to look her in the eye. It forced Jennifer to ask a question that made her blood run cold. "Aisha, how much do you remember?"

"I remember *everything,* Jennifer. You let Emerick into our lives even after knowing what he was and lied to me. Of all the years I've known you, you never once told me what you were. Not until…"

"…I'm sorry, Aisha. But…"

Aisha raised her hand to silence her. Her tone and movements were all deliberate and lacking emotion. It was different to possession.

Aisha seemed *broken.*

"I'm done with your lying, Jennifer. I just want answers. You're a witch, I get that part. Your mom, too. Emerick and Ambrose were demons… Is that right?"

Jennifer nodded, then confirmed it out loud so there would be no more misunderstandings.

"Yes. All true."

"So, what happened with Sebastian? What was he and how did he die?"

Jennifer peered over at Lobo resting by Sebastian's closed casket, alongside Fernando.

It was empty, of course. But the wolf was smart, Jennifer knew that he understood. She turned back to Aisha. "Sebastian is... Sebastian *was* a werewolf. Gremory took his soul to hell."

Aisha pursed her lips together and nodded.

She turned her gaze to Daniella and Chelsea who were sitting on the grass, talking amongst themselves.

"And Daniella is pregnant with Sebastian's child," Aisha remarked.

"You know?" Jennifer asked.

"I do. Will her child be...?"

"Yes. Their child will be another Colby wolf. Just like the rest of their bloodline."

"*Another* wolf? Wow."

There was a crippling silence, which Jennifer felt the need to make up for.

"I'm pregnant too," Jennifer added.

The very first hint of emotion filled Aisha's face since they had started talking.

But Jennifer couldn't place the emotion. Was it pity? Happiness? Jennifer couldn't be sure.

"You?"

"Yes."

"To Emerick or Sebastian?"

Tongue in cheek, Jennifer felt the shame of her friend asking such a question. "Emerick."

"Oh, so your child will be part witch part demon spawn... I guess it's a good thing I'm leaving Richmont because the last thing I need in my life is more of the hell we've just gone through."

"You can't be serious!"

"I'm very serious. You once told me that Ambrose and Emerick were monsters, and I didn't believe you then. But now, that I'm aware of everything, I'm just glad to be rid of the worst monster of all... The girl I thought was my best friend."

"Aisha, you don't mean..."

Before Jennifer could finish her sentence, Aisha stormed away. Jennifer went to chase her, but she was stopped by Marian and Fernando.

"Jennifer," Marian began. "Fernando would like..."

"I can speak for myself, Marian," Fernando interrupted. Jennifer could smell the whiskey on his breath, but considering what he was going through, she understood.

Alas, Fernando continued to address Jennifer.

"I want you to know I don't blame you for Sebastian's death."

"Thank you," Jennifer said. Fernando glanced briefly over his shoulder at Lobo who was making his way towards them, before turning back to her. "I understand Lobo thinks highly of you. Which is why... I hope you will look after him."

Jennifer could see by the pain in the man's eyes just what the act of giving up Lobo meant to him. And as Lobo brushed his head against the side of her leg it made her realize the brutal realization of the moment.

She stammered to speak.

"What... What do you mean?"

"As Sebastian's soulmate and Lobo's witch, he belongs with you. Please... Please look after him for..." As Fernando gave into his grief on Marian's shoulder, Jennifer's breath escaped her.

Sebastian's soulmate? Those words hit just as hard as the realization did.

She crumbled to her knees and sobbed into Lobo's black fur.

While that day she had been forced to say 'goodbye' to her two best friends, at least she wouldn't be alone.

✳ ✳ ✳

While Jennifer took it upon herself to bring Daniella ambrosia tea each day, she divulged the entire secret of the Morris-Colby curse.

At first, Daniella had been so mad, but eventually that anger settled and soon she grew accustomed to having Lobo accompany Jennifer on her visits.

As per Marian's request, Emerick had remained a guest at the Morris household, however, it wasn't until two weeks after the funeral, that Jennifer finally spoke to him. Her silence had been for a number of reasons. But at the top of that list was the guilt she felt for how complicated her life was. She found Emerick deep in thought, sitting on his bed with the amulet in his hands.

"You're not having second thoughts of trapping him in there, are you?" she asked.

"No. I was just thinking that maybe I should be in here with him."

Jennifer sat on the bed beside him. "You're not to blame, Emerick. Besides, we saved all the souls that were taken by Gremory."

Emerick took her hand in his. "All but one."

"Yeah," she paused to process her thoughts. "What hurts the most is that he went to hell with Gremory because of me."

"You truly love him, don't you?"

Jennifer nodded. "I didn't want to. We both tried to move on, but it's because of our love for each other that this happened."

Those words were like static in the air. She knew what he was thinking. She knew how he felt about her. But there was nothing she could do to change what had happened nor how she felt.

"If it's any consolation, I'm sorry, Jennifer. I'm sorry for lying and I'm sorry for getting you into this mess. But, if I may, can I ask you something?" She held eye contact with him.

But her expression was vacant. "What do you need to ask me?"

"How much of our time were you, you, and not Gremory?"

Jennifer considered his question. "I was me when we first met. When we first kissed... When we... When we made love. That was me. I did fall for you pretty hard. I was ready to have something normal with you. But I also..."

"...Your heart belonged to Sebastian."

"Maybe that's all because of curse between our families, but yes, it did."

There was a long, loud silence. Jennifer and Emerick could've had something real.

Or maybe not. Maybe Jennifer was just fated to have bad luck in love like every other Morris witch. Still, she mustered her courage to look to the future. She had to.

"We can't change the past, Emerick but we can look to the future. I'm carrying a child that's part Morris witch, part succubus. And thanks to my genetics, she'll even have a little angel in her too. A witch, demon, angel tri-bred."

"A girl? How do you know?"

"It's part of the Morris Curse. We can't have boys like the Colby's do. I'm surprised we haven't died out."

Emerick passed the amulet to Jennifer. "You should have this."

"No, after what happened. I can't..."

"...Gremory isn't in it anymore. You sent her to hell."

"That's not the point. Besides, you need it."

"Not as much as our daughter is going to need it. What about when she grows of age and has her first kiss? She's going to need to devour souls. There's no way around it."

"Oh, she won't be kissing…"

The look Emerick gave brought a chuckle to Jennifer's throat. Of course, her daughter would need to devour souls. Unless there was some spell she could weave. Or some loophole.

But unfortunately, she would be both a Morris Witch and a succubus. Jennifer wouldn't even be able to send her daughter to a convent.

Reluctantly, Jennifer took the amulet.

"Alright. I'll give it to her… Eventually. What are you going to do to fulfill your own needs?"

Emerick got to his feet and held out his hand to her. "I'm going to offer myself up as a sacrifice. Me for Sebastian. And you're going to help."

Was that even possible? Could he actually bring back Sebastian? And if he did, what condition would Sebastian be in?

There were so many rules in Marian's spell book telling of the dangers of necromancy. But none of them spoke of sacrificing one soul for another. Most likely because nobody wanted to sacrifice themselves at all. "Are you sure about this?"

"I've been to hell more times than I can remember. I'll be fine."

TWENTY-ONE

Barrett Manor stood in ruins before Jennifer, Emerick and Lobo. "You can always back out of this plan at any time," Jennifer said. "You were the first woman I've been with for a very long time," Emerick replied. "And you'll continue to be the only woman for me until my dying breath. But love means sacrifice. So let me be the sacrifice that brings Sebastian back."

"So much for your hatred towards teen romance novels."

"What can I say? You converted me."

Jennifer took Emerick's hand and the two entered the old building. Traces of blood lined the walls, shattered glass rested on every floor and surface. It seemed nobody dared clean the mess. The very atmosphere made Jennifer sick to her stomach. They trailed up the steps, down the corridor to the right, and towards the room that she and Sebastian had made love.

As Emerick stepped into the room and Lobo sniffed around at the bed, Jennifer felt compelled to stand out in the hallway.

"It's okay," Emerick said. "Come in when you're ready."

After a further hesitation, Jennifer mustered her courage and entered. She sat opposite Emerick in the middle of the pentagram on the rug, then took two black candles and her mother's spell book from her backpack. She blew a small puff of air on to the wick of the first candle, igniting the the flame, then used that one to light up the second.

"Impressive," Emerick remarked.

"Thank you. Are you ready?"

"Whenever you are."

Jennifer flicked through the pages searching for the right spell. She was nowhere near ready. How could she be ready to send somebody to hell?

It just didn't make sense. Her fingers began to shake, until Emerick took them in his own hands.

"It's okay. You've got this."

"Oh, right. Should I like... kiss you goodbye or something...?"

He looked at her, amused.

Of course, she couldn't kiss him. She no longer possessed the immunity to incubi. But she still had so many questions. Like how would she raise a succubus? What age would her daughter be when she first needed to devour a soul?

She knew her mother would be able to help, but these were questions that nobody could answer.

After she had found the spell that Emerick had given her before they had left the house, nodded at

Emerick and closed her eyes ready to begin her chant. "I invoke the will of Hekate, upon the power of the Morris lineage. Guided by Hermes and the devil, Lucifer. I offer up a trade.

The soldier, Emerick of the twenty-first legion of Gremory for the soul of Sebastian Colby. Give me what I seek!"

Jennifer opened her eyes. Emerick was still sitting there. The candles were still lit.

"Go again," Emerick said. So, she did. Only louder this time.

"I invoke the will of Hekate, upon the power of the Morris lineage. Guided by Hermes and the devil, Lucifer. I offer up a trade. The soldier, Emerick of the twenty-first legion of Gremory for the soul of Sebastian Colby. Give me what I seek!"

The candles flickered. The chandelier above Emerick began to sway and the clouds began to darken. This time Jennifer yelled with full emotion.

"I invoke the will of Hekate, upon the power of the Morris lineage. Guided by Hermes and the devil, Lucifer, himself. I offer up a trade. The soldier, Emerick of the twenty-first legion of Gremory for the soul of Sebastian Colby. Give me what I seek!"

Upon those words, the candle flames disappeared, and the chandelier came crashing down. With a scream, Jennifer jumped out of the way to escape the shattering glass.

But Emerick was gone. Jennifer looked around. As did Lobo.

Neither were sure if the spell had worked. A chilling breeze ran across her face, but ultimately, she was alone. Taking her things, and her wolf Jennifer left, never to step foot in Barrett Manor again.

✳✳✳

Days passed by and Jennifer couldn't help but wonder if she had been fooled by Emerick.

Occasionally, sometimes she would thumb the amulet in her hand, watching the blur of smoke pass by the glass. But she never stopped thinking about Sebastian. She couldn't help but consider how Lobo felt. Sure, he had been her soulmate, but Sebastian and Lobo had shared a body.

One night, when Jennifer was curled up on the couch with Lobo watching television, the wolf was alerted to a disturbance outside. He scratched and whined at the door until Jennifer opened it.

The moment she did, Lobo bolted outside faster than she could run after him.

"Lobo! Lobo, come back!" she called as she chased after him in the dark street.

The wolf ran until he was stopped by a large invisible force, which ignite a deep howl right.

And as Lobo howled, he transformed... into Sebastian. Jennifer's eyes grew wide. He was naked and his hair was scruffy. And there was a pain in his eyes which haunted her. She raced towards him, pulling him into a very tight embrace, and relaxed as he buried his nose into her neck and sobbed.

Remembering that he was naked in the cold street, Jennifer led him into the house.

✳✳✳

"I'm so glad you're back!" Jennifer said, after she had assisted Sebastian into some of Emerick's old clothes. But as ecstatic as she felt to see him, she struggled to comprehend the right words, or the appropriate actions to react to the situation.

They sat together on the couch in silence, as Sebastian refused to speak of what he had been through. When he did finally speak, his words were simply, "thank you for looking after Lobo."

"I think it was more him looking after me. He refused to sleep unless he was curled up beside me. I'll miss having him around."

"I wish I could do the same."

She could tell by the faint smile etched across his lips, that he was desperately trying to lighten the mood. She thought back to the scars she had seen on Emerick's back and wondered if Sebastian had endured the same fate. That thought made her think of Emerick. Of the fact that he had traded places with Sebastian, willingly. She ached just to think about it. "Do you want some tea?" she asked, referring to one of her mother's herbals.

Sebastian gave a simple gesture, as if he was afraid to say 'yes' out of fear of what might happen. While Jennifer had prayed this day would come, she had underestimated the emotions it would dredge up in her. She supported him into the kitchen and made them some calming herbal tea.

As they drank, Jennifer told him everything, but most importantly, she revealed that Gremory was gone. But she did so, cautiously. For she knew was far more broken in comparison to the one she had lost. This one was more silent, more cautious, more hesitant. Jennifer had just finished telling him about Emerick's sacrifice, when Sebastian asked,

"How is Daniella?" Of course, he would ask about Daniella. She was the mother to his unborn child.

"She misses you. Don't worry, I filled her in about the whole Morris-Colby curse. We've been trying to work on a solution to prevent our babies from ever having to suffer through what we've gone through."

"Do you think that's possible?"

"I'm not sure. But I'm willing to stop at nothing to try. The problem is, I might be onto a solution."

"Why is that a problem?"

While she hadn't spoken her theory out loud to anybody yet, Sebastian was the only person in the world that she would tell.

"I was thinking that maybe we keep them separated from magic. Don't let my daughter know that your family are wolves, and that she's part witch, part succubus. Just keep it all a secret."

"How would that even work?"

Sebastian's confusion had been expected. In fact, Jennifer expected that her mother would not take the idea well at all. But Jennifer believed she was onto something.

"Well, you see, while I have the gift of magic, it's my belief in the craft that makes it work. It's my emotions that fuel the spell. If my daughter doesn't believe in magic, then she won't be able to use magic." Sebastian nodded slowly. He agreed. But there were some complications that they both saw.

"If I'm to keep my wolf curse a secret from her, that means you and I won't be able to be together. Our children won't be allowed to know each other."

Jennifer knew that already.

That was the part that hurt the most.

He closed his eyes as his dark eyelashes soaked up the tears that had emerged.

Then, giving into his own grief, he brought her hand to his lips and landed a kiss. Jennifer pulled him into her arms, as he sobbed softly on her shoulder. "It's okay, Sebastian. I'm going to make you forget how you feel about me, okay?"

"You tried that, remember? It didn't work."

"No, that was an unlove spell. I might not be able to stop myself from loving you, but I can make you forget how you feel about me."

Sebastian pulled his head away and nodded.

"Can we not do it tonight? I just... Tonight, I just want to sleep beside you. Please."

They were the words that Jennifer so desperately needed to hear. She brought him up to her bedroom and curled into his arms under her covers, in the dim light.

The moment brought them back to their times as a couple. To their times as children.

"I missed you," Sebastian said, stroking her hair. "That place... it was... it was *hell*. I was tortured. Beaten. Burned... I was..."

Jennifer couldn't bear him reliving the pain. It was because of her that he had endured any of it. She needed to give him something to make it all better. She kissed him and Sebastian was lulled into silence. She tried to pull away, but Sebastian held her and kissed her back with all his strength. Their emotions took a hold and the more they kissed, the more their passion grew.

Soon, they were both bare of all clothing and giving into their own desires for one another. But while it was normally Sebastian who took the lead, this time it was Jennifer.

She wanted to take away all his pain, all his torment and replace it with the insatiable love that she felt for him. And so, she did.

✳✳✳

In the early hours of the morning, Jennifer sat opposite Sebastian on the couch. While neither of them truly wanted to do the Forget spell, they knew it was for the best, and after, there would be no turning back. After having mentally prepared herself, Jennifer peered into his eyes and started her spell. "Sebastian Lucas Colby, I love you. I always have and I always will. But you and I, we can't be together. Because when we do that, there's only pain, death, and sorrow. So, I need you to forget that you love me. Forget that you would be willing to die for me... And most of all, forget just how much it is that I love you. Because I just can't lose you again." Following her words, Jennifer kissed him one last time.

As Sebastian came to his senses, the enthusiasm he seemed to have lost so long ago, returned.

He wiped the tears from his face, got to his feet and grinned, "Wow, Morris. How the hell am I going to tell my parents that I'm back from the dead?"

"You could just walk in all casual and act like nothing happened."

Sebastian's smile reached his eyes for the first time in what seemed like forever. "Perfect plan. I bet mom will freak. I'll see you back at school, alright?" Jennifer followed him towards the front door, faking her smile.

"Just make sure you say 'hi' to Daniella for me, okay?"

"I will." Then he hugged her. Probably a little longer than he should have.

Suddenly, the front door opened to reveal Marian standing in the doorway. She had spent the entire night out with Sheriff Mike again.

At Marian's sudden arrival, Sebastian, and Jennifer broke their embrace as Marian's eyes opened wide in surprise. However, she held her tongue until after Sebastian had left.

"What did you do, Jennifer?"

"I didn't do anything. It was Emerick. He sacrificed himself to bring back Sebastian."

Marian shook her head. "He's not the only one to have made a sacrifice, Jennifer. You cast a Forget spell on Sebastian, didn't you?"

"How did you know?"

"Why do you think Fernando and I hate each other?"

In that moment, Marian's bitter relationship with Sebastian's father made sense. And Jennifer had just repeated that same mistake.

TWENTY-TWO

Richmont, 2013

Seven-year-old Briana Morris sat in the reading corner of the classroom surrounded by shelves of books, toys, games and jigsaw puzzles. But she wasn't focused on any of those activities. Oh no. She had her heart set on the blue pack of playing cards. Her grandma had taught her a new trick. Sure, her mom would be mad if she found out, but it didn't make Briana any less interested to give it a try.

She took the pack of playing cards from the shelf and was about to pour them onto the blue carpet, when she was startled by a boy coming to sit with her. He had dark hair, dark eyes and a button-like nose which crinkled up when he smiled. "Can I sit with you?" he asked.

His question surprised her. Simply because none of the other kids ever wanted to go near her. It was almost as if they were afraid of her, and she didn't understand why. Briana shrugged. "Sure. But won't the other kids make fun of you?"

"They do that anyway. They think I'm weird. What's your name?"

Briana took the cards out of the pack and started shuffling the same way her grandma had taught her. Careful not to mess them up. "Briana Morris," she said, not removing her eyes from the cards. She didn't want to lose focus. If she lost focus it would mess up her trick entirely.

"I'm Lucas Colby. What game did you want to play?"

Briana shook her head. "I'm not playing. I'm practicing. My grandma says we can't lose focus when doing magic."

The word 'magic' stole his attention entirely.

"A magic trick? Like a magician?"

Briana grinned. "Exactly like a magician. Only a girl magician. We're prettier. Did you want to see?"

Lucas nodded, excited. But said nothing.

"Well, we can't show anybody else. Do you swear?" She held up her pinkie finger. He linked his through hers.

"I swear."

"Good."

As they unlinked fingers, Lucas sat back, ready to see the magic trick, while Briana split the deck in half and held both piles faced down in each of her hands. "Are you ready?" she asked.

"Uh huh!" he was very excited. Briana checked to see that nobody was watching. The coast was clear.

She took a slight breath in, focused, and allowed her magic to do the rest.

The cards floated up into the air, slowly spreading out in a delightful display. Lucas's eyes went wide as he applauded. "Wow! That's so cool!"

Enjoying the attention, Briana decided to pull her second trick. "If you think that's cool, you should see this part." Lucas sat up on his knees, unsure how the trick could get any better.

"Now, for my next trick," Briana said adopting a tone that one might recognized in a skilled magician. "I need you to think of a card. Any card. Don't tell me what it is, okay?"

"Okay, I know the card. It's my favorite."

Briana smiled then turned her attention back to the floating cards. She ran her fingers through the gaps between the cards.

Then, while a vast majority of them floated facedown onto the carpet, seven cards remained face down in the air. Briana turned her attention back to Lucas. "I predict that your card is one of these. Are you ready?"

"Yes. I bet you can't guess it."

"I bet I can," Briana argued. She hovered her hand over each of the cards until she got to the fifth card. She turned it over, careful not to show Lucas. It was the ace of hearts. As she held it in her hand, the rest of the cards fell to the carpet.

"I have your card, Lucas."

"What is it?" he asked. Briana studied it.

But this was the first time she had ever been able to show her magic to somebody else besides her grandma. She couldn't even show her magic to her mom.

The very thought of having a friend that she could share secrets with and be herself with was far too exciting. She wanted to impress him more.

"Just one more trick, okay?"

He nodded with that big grin spread across his face. She waved her hand and the card disappeared into midair.

Lucas gasped. "Where did it go?"

"Not in my sleeves," Briana giggled, showing him the cuffs of her pink hoodie. "Why don't you check your sleeves?"

Lucas checked his sleeves.

In pure amazement, he pulled the card from his right sleeve. "That's so cool!" he said, struggling to contain his excitement.

But Briana began to second guess herself. "That was your card, right? Ace of hearts?"

"Yes. My dad said it's a girl card, but I like it."

"It's my favorite too. But I need you to promise that you will not tell anybody about that trick, okay? It needs to be our secret."

"I promise. Friends?"

Again, he held up his pinkie finger. Briana couldn't resist. She linked her finger through his. "Friends forever."

The smile that spread across her face could light up a room. She had just made her first friend and she couldn't wait to tell her mom.

❋ ❋ ❋

At four pm, Jennifer bustled through the front door of her quaint home and set her purse and keys down on the coffee table. She was exhausted from working the day shift at the hospital, but she still needed to get dinner on the table before Andrew got home. She had an hour and a half until then.

Her mom would've already picked Briana up from school, which would give her enough time to shower and get dinner started.

She hated cooking. It was times like that when she wished she had never made that vow to cut magic from her life. She hated cutting the onions.

She hated the time it took. She hated burning herself on the frying pan every single time.

But most of all, she hated how it was never to Andrew's standards. Nothing ever was.

Sometimes she wondered why she even bothered. But that was the life she had chosen.

And Jennifer vowed that that night she would at least try to make a decent meal.

She showered for ten minutes, dressed then checked her face in the mirror.

The water had washed away the makeup that hid the bruise to her right eye. Surely just a little magic could remove it completely.

She really didn't want Briana to see. As she brought her fingertips to her face, she was startled by a knock at the door. Too late.

Instead, she combed her hair over her face to cover it up and headed to the living room to open the front door. If Marian knew he had done it again, there would be all hell to pay. Literally, in fact. Marian hated Andrew with a passion. But Jennifer didn't need Marian's lectures. She wasn't a kid anymore. She made her own choices.

Jennifer breathed out and opened the door. But it wasn't Marian that was standing there. Nor had Andrew come home early.

Instead, she stood face to face with the man she hadn't seen in several years. And he was just as handsome as she remembered.

Sebastian was dressed in a red business shirt rolled up to his elbows, black pants, and he looked just as surprised as she was to be there.

"Ah, hi, Sebastian," she fumbled. "What are...? What are you doing here?"

"Can we talk?" Every instinct in her gut told her to say 'no'. It was wrong on so many levels.

"I probably shouldn't. Andrew will be home soon and..."

But Sebastian stormed into the house anyway. After ensuring that her hair was still hiding the bruise to her eye, Jennifer invited him to sit, and closed the door behind them. But neither of them could sit. Nervousness loomed in the air.

"You said we needed to talk?" she asked.

"Oh, ah... Right. So, our kids met each other today. Lucas said Briana's his first friend."

Jennifer groaned. While it was great news that Briana had finally made a friend. Why did it have to be a Colby boy?

It was no wonder why Sebastian had come to her house. They needed to stop the children's friendship before it blossomed into something more. "I'm so sorry, Sebastian. I'll speak with..."

"...No, don't do that." The moment he cut her off, his hand fell to her shoulder in support, but her reaction was to brush him away. And as she did, her hair fell away from her eye, revealing the bruise she had been hiding. As his attention focused on the bruise, Jennifer could sense his anger building. "That *his* handiwork?" he snarled.

"Let it go, Sebastian."

"How can I when you're letting some dirtbag mortal beat on you? You're stronger than this, Jennifer! So, act like it."

"Quit telling me what to do. You have no say in this house, so just tell me what you came here for."

The last thing she needed was him telling her how to live. She had given him up so that he could live a happy life with Daniella and their children.

Not so he could come into her house and act like he was concerned for her wellbeing.

Sebastian opened his mouth ready to argue but changed his mind at the last minute.

"Fine. I'm not saying we need to break the children's friendship. Just... Is there some way to alter the Morris-Colby curse? Maybe even end it?"

The question Jennifer had searched her entire life for. Her ancestor, Rose Morris had created the curse out of heartbreak. And all parties had been inflicted. As had their descendants.

The only answer would be to move away from each other, but their descendants would always find a way back to one another.

On her silence, Sebastian continued. "You once said magic doesn't work if you don't believe in it. Maybe we could just stop believing in the curse?" On his theory, Jennifer invited him to sit with her on the couch. This time, he did.

"It's not that easy. If you don't believe you're a wolf, does that stop you from turning into a wolf?" He shook his head. But he wasn't done trying.

"Your mother believed we could stop the curse, don't you remember?"

The fact that he remembered that part made her miss the past. How he could just lighten the mood by bringing it up was torturous. But Marian's idea had been absurd.

"Yeah," Jennifer chuckled. "She thought that the answer to the curse would be you and

me getting married and having a baby."

"Could that even work?"

The fact that he was even considering it was a very bad idea for more reasons than one.

He was married and she was with Andrew. They had their own lives. Then there was the part that he had already died for her once. This time there would be no Emerick willing to sacrifice himself for Sebastian's soul. She went to argue, but he was already in the middle of his own trail of thought.

"It's hard to believe that no Colby has ever gotten a Morris pregnant. Especially because both our families are very well-known for our prowess."

His smile told her exactly what memory was on his mind. But Jennifer needed to keep the matter professional. She positioned herself further away from him on the couch and said, "I've studied the curse extensively. There's been some journal entries left behind. There were a few steamy activities undertaken by some of our ancestors. But none resulted in any babies. You also weren't the first Colby to die for... well... the curse. But you were the only one that came back from the dead."

His eyes closed briefly, the moment she said curse. "I didn't die for the curse, Jennifer. I died for loving you too much. My wolf spirit was fighting to take hold of my body. I should've transformed while we were in that bed. But in that moment, I needed to stay me, for you. And so, I was strong enough to overcome my own transformation because of how much I loved you."

Her blood grew cold. "No... it was..."

"...Argue as much as you want, but it was love. It wasn't until two minutes ago when I saw you, that I remembered how you made me forget. But honestly, I'd go to hell and back for you again, if I had to."

"Don't say that" Jennifer stammered. "We…"

"…I know. We're over. And I was supposed to come here to talk about our children and if we can find a way to alter the curse. So maybe we should just get back to doing that then, huh?"

Jennifer got to her feet, fearing what she might do if she continued to sit beside him.

"Yes, Sebastian. Let's do that. Like I was saying, my mom believed we were supposed to have a baby. But I don't know how when our ancestors have tried in the past. I can't understand a scientific reason behind it because they've always gone on to have children with other partners."

Sebastian leaned back on the couch. His eyes rested on a photo frame of Jennifer and Briana, before scanning the many other photos around the room, some of which had Marian in them.

"I need to ask, why are there no photos of that spineless creep, of yours?"

"That's not nice to say."

But Sebastian didn't care. He stood and approached her. "No, what's not nice is that every time I look at that bruise on your face, I have to control myself not to transform and shred that son of a bitch's limb from limb."

"Sebastian? If you keep speaking like that, I swear to the goddess that I will banish you from my house and you will never be welcomed here again. Do you understand?"

He hunched his shoulders and offered a disgruntled nod.

"Alright, fine. So, I guess babies are out of the question."

"Wait, what?"

"I'm talking about the curse."

His eyes lingered right back to the bruise on her eye, and he bit into his lower lip to hold back another angry opinion.

"I'm sorry, but I can't stay here any longer."

He charged past her and brought his hand to the door. But before he could open it, he turned back. "Find some way to break that curse, Jennifer, because I sure as hell won't let my son suffer for our mistakes. I'd rather die first... again."

"Our mistake? The curse wasn't our mistake. It was..."

Before she could finish her sentence, he pulled her head to his and kissed her. Jennifer's entire body trembled. Her knees went weak. But before she could kiss him back, he pulled away.

"That was for... well, it doesn't matter anymore."

He opened the door and went to leave, only to see Jennifer's current boyfriend, Andrew standing in the doorway dressed in an expensive grey business suit. Great animosity loomed in the air between them, and Jennifer had no choice but to improvise her way out of the complicated situation.

"Oh, hi, Andrew. This is Sebastian Colby... Ah, he's... Briana's *teacher*. And he just came to tell me that Briana made a new friend. Isn't that great?"

Both men looked to her in surprise.

"Her teacher?" Andrew asked. She could tell by his tone that he didn't believe her. "I thought her teacher's name was Miss Jude?"

Of course, he had paid attention to that part. Normally Andrew didn't care about anything that concerned Briana. Before Jennifer could improvise again, Sebastian held out his hand to Andrew.

"That's right," Sebastian said. "Miss Jude is normally Briana's teacher. But I substituted the class today and Miss Jude informed me that Briana has been struggling in the friends' department and that Jennifer here, has been a little concerned."

Thankful for his lie, Jennifer allowed herself to breathe a little. "Well, she is a strange child," Andrew laughed. Though neither he, nor Sebastian broke their handshake. Sebastian's grip tightened, forcing Andrew's hand to redden.

"She's actually a very bright child. I think the other students might just be a little bit intimidated. Andrew, was it?"

"Yes. Andrew Crow. I manage the Richmont bank." It didn't take a mastermind to realize that a grade A macho contest was being had in her very doorway. Jennifer needed to break it up, before one of them got hurt. Namely Andrew.

Surprisingly, Sebastian released Andrew's hand.

"Well, it was nice to meet you, Andrew. I hope to see you again, soon."

Andrew kneaded his knuckles. "Jennifer, why don't you see him to his car?"

Jennifer led Sebastian to the brand-new silver Mazda parked on the road at the front of her house. "I see you traded in your jag," she said, trying to lighten the mood.

"Lose him," Sebastian snarled.

"What?"

"You heard me. Because if he hurts you or your daughter, again, the next news report you hear will be that that man was mauled to death by a pack of angry wolves. And that's a promise."

With that last remark, Sebastian got into his car and sped off down the road.

TWENTY-THREE

Jennifer awoke to the terrorized screams of Briana down the hall. In the bed beside Jennifer, Andrew brought his pillow to his head and rolled over. Good. She didn't want his help anyway. After having brought her feet to the floor, Jennifer tiptoed towards Briana's bedroom.

The moment she opened the door, she was met by Briana running into her arms, horrified. "Briana? What's the matter? What happened?" But Briana simply pointed to her closet.

"Mommy, there's a monster in my cupboard."

While most parents who suffered that same problem with their children night after night, were all able to assure their kids that there were no such things as monsters, Jennifer knew the truth.

Of course, monsters existed. However, as Jennifer did her nightly monster-hunt, she knew without a doubt that there were no monsters in Briana's bedroom. And thanks to all the protection charms that secretly lined the house, no monsters or demons could get in, either. The only monster Jennifer could think of was currently asleep in her bed. But that was a whole different story.

"See, Briana?" Jennifer said, pointing into the wardrobe.

"No monsters. There's none under your bed. None in the closet and there's none anywhere else in the house."

But poor Briana would not release Jennifer's hand for a second.

"Can you sleep in my bed, mommy? In case the monster comes back?"

Jennifer considered the alternative and agreed to Briana almost immediately. "Of course, baby."

As the two settled into the small bed, Briana brought her hand to Jennifer's bruised eye and accidentally brushed past the fresh sore on her lip.

Andrew's latest handiwork for Jennifer inviting Sebastian Colby into the home.

"It's okay, mommy. You're all better now." Hearing those words sent Jennifer through a mental whiplash. With her hand, Jennifer checked her eye and then her lip. The bruises were gone. Briana had healed them. But that was impossible. Jennifer had been careful not to let Briana learn magic.

Just then Jennifer realized just who was responsible. Marian Morris.

But if Marian had been teaching Briana to believe in magic, then what else was possible? Jennifer's eyes rested on the closet.

✳ ✳ ✳

The next day was Thursday, which was Jennifer's rostered day off. And while normally she loved working as a nurse to get her mind off her personal life, Jennifer had plans for that day. After she dropped Briana off at school, she made her way over to her mother's house. She rarely visited these days, mostly because it took her right back to her childhood.

Before she could even knock, the front door opened in front of her. Clearly, Marian was expecting her. She stepped into the house taking in every sight, smell, and memory one by one.

She remembered her times with Sebastian. Aisha. Emerick. And even that horrible night at Barrett Manor.

She climbed the steps and headed to her mother's summoning room to see her mother sitting at the crystal ball table.

"I thought I sensed you pull up. What's the matter?"

Jennifer took the seat across from her and got straight to business. "I need you to stop teaching Briana magic. She's seven and she believes in closet monsters. Have you any idea how dangerous that is?"

"Sure, it's dangerous. But it's not nearly half as dangerous as her having no idea how to control her own magic. She's not a normal girl, Jennifer, stop treating her like she is."

"Yes, she is, mom. She's seven years old. She's still struggling to make friends at school.

Hell, if it wasn't for Sebastian's son..."

"...Sebastian's son?" That piqued Marian's interest. She hovered her hands over the crystal ball, while Jennifer continued to talk.

"Yes. His name is Lucas. None of the other kids want to be their friends because they think they're weird."

With Marian's focus on the crystal ball, Jennifer felt a little uneasy. What the hell was her mother reading with such fascination?

Until finally, Marian spoke up, without shifting her focus.

"You're here about the Morris-Colby curse, aren't you?"

"That's a part of it. Sebastian visited me, yesterday. Asked me to…"

"…He visited you at the house?" That piqued Marian's attention even more. A devious smile flashed across her face. "I'm sure Andrew wasn't too pleased. Did you and Sebastian have sex?"

And there was the reason Jennifer refused to speak to her mother about anything.

"This is ridiculous. Sebastian is still married to Daniella. I'm with Andrew." She stood up, ready to leave.

"Not for long," Marian said shifting her focus from the ball to Jennifer, encouraging her to sit back down.

She did, as Marian continued speaking. "Andrew won't survive the week. But you and Briana have other matters to contend with and I'm sorry for my part in it. But remember, whatever you choose to do, I'll always love you."

"What are you...?"

"Oh, and the Morris-Colby curse will soon come to an end."

"It will? When?"

Marian turned her focus back to the ball, waved her hand over it again then frowned.

"Oh, such a pity I won't be around to see it."

Jennifer did a double take. That was an information overload while at the same time being just too vague.

And unfortunately, Marian refused to divulge any more information than she already had.

To Jennifer's frustration, she had come for answers, but left with only more questions.

✳ ✳ ✳

Marian's predictions had left Jennifer out of sorts for the rest of the day. While she spent the rest of the afternoon cooking and cleaning, she theorized just what Marian might've meant. Evidently, Marian had hinted that Andrew wouldn't survive the week. Did that have something to do with what Sebastian had said? Surely, Sebastian wouldn't stoop so low as to kill a mortal for her.

"Are you coming to bed or not?" Andrew asked as she dressed into her pajamas that night.

"Oh, uh… Yeah," she stammered.

She didn't want to. He had been drinking.

She hated how he got when he drank. Still, she crawled under the covers beside him.

In minutes his hands were on her body, his lips were on her mouth. He tasted disgusting. Nothing like Sebastian, whose lips had been on her memory since he had kissed her the day before. But before Andrew could push the moment any further, they were alerted to the guttural scream of Briana. But tonight, the scream was different. More desperate.

Jennifer pulled back, ready to run to her daughter's aide, but Andrew merely pulled her back to him.

"No, Jennifer. Come here. Forget her."

Jennifer tried to kiss him. Tried to allow herself to jot Briana's cries down to nothing more than her imagination, just to satisfy Andrew's urges.

But when Briana screamed again, she just couldn't bear it. She attempted the climb out of the bed, only to have Andrew pull her straight in again and climb onto her.

"You're not going anywhere, Jennifer."

"No, get off me!"

"I'm trying to get off."

"GET OFF!" she shouted, forcing him to fly backwards out of the bed, giving her the chance to make her getaway.

Jennifer fled from the bed and rushed into Briana's room only to be met by a sight that frightened her more than the night that Gremory stole Sebastian's soul. Briana sat terrified in her bed. Her blanket pulled up to her chin as she watched her very own wardrobe burn from the inside. Amongst the flames stood what could only be described as the silhouette of a horned demon.

"Oh, my goddess!" Jennifer stammered.

As Andrew rushed into the room behind her, horrified by the sight, she knew that it was not just the imagination of her child that she had been suckered into.

On impulse, Jennifer ripped Briana from her bed as Andrew just stood in wide-eyed terror.

"Come on, Andrew!" she cried, leading them out of the house, trying to come to terms with what they had just seen.

"What the hell was that?!" Andrew yelled at Jennifer, despite the fact she still had Briana in her arms. "I don't know!" Jennifer placed Briana on the floor beside her. "But it didn't look like the fire was spreading."

"You caused this, didn't you? You and your goddamn daughter!"

"Don't you ever talk that way about me and my daughter, again. Of course, I didn't cause it."

"You didn't? Because I beg to differ. You know what everybody thinks of you in this town, right?

They think you're a witch. You and that demon spawn of yours."

"Mommy, what is daddy talking about?" Briana asked.

"Nothing, baby. He was just being silly. Weren't you, Andrew?" But the anger in Andrew's eyes was evident that he didn't care if Briana heard him or not. He turned to the child and said, "No, I wasn't being silly. Your mom has been..."

Before Andrew could finish his sentence, a large black wolf leaped onto him from out of nowhere, growling in protection of Jennifer and Briana. Lobo.

"Mom, it's a dog!" Briana shrilled in delight.

"Lobo, off!" Jennifer ordered, and the wolf willingly obeyed.

Andrew got to his feet. "What... What the...?" But he didn't finish his sentence. He turned and fled.

Lobo transformed into Sebastian almost immediately and Briana gasped in amazement.

"You seriously shouldn't have done that, Sebastian!" Jennifer snapped.

"Really? Lobo heard you scream from my house, and you get mad at me. So typical, Jennifer. What the hell happened?"

While Jennifer refused to say anything, Briana took the lead of the conversation.

"There's a monster in my closet and this time my mommy and my daddy saw it too."

Sebastian's reaction was equally instantaneous as it was filled with adorable enthusiasm.

"Oh, really? That sounds scary. Are you okay?"

Briana nodded. "Yeah, a little scared though."

"I bet."

Jennifer rolled her eyes. "It was literally her imagination of closet monsters manifested as a demon. And this is why I'm taking her to my mom's house for a goddam forget magic spell. I'm assuming you can walk home from here."

Without another word, Jennifer, packed Briana into the car and drove to her mom's house.

"You're welcome, by the way." Sebastian called out. But his eyes lingered on Andrew who had raced off in the distance.

✳ ✳ ✳

For the rest of the night, Jennifer sat up speaking with her mother, while Briana slept in Jennifer's old bedroom. Although Marian refused to hear it, Jennifer was adamant that Briana needed to forget about magic. "But what about when Briana tries to have her first kiss?" Marian asked. "We should be able to prepare her for…"

"No, mom. To hell with first kisses. If my daughter keeps going the way she's going, she won't even make it to her teenaged years."

"Well, we can teach her to protect herself how to…" Marian stopped speaking as Jennifer's attention was brought to the television in the kitchen, which was presenting a picture of Andrew.

"Woah mom, turn that up!" Marian pointed her hand at the television, immediately switching up the volume.

"Officers have been brought to the scene where the remains of Richmont bank manager, Andrew Crow have been discovered tonight. It is suspected that Andrew was torn apart by wolves."

"Oh, my goddess! Andrew is very well known." Jennifer groaned. She knew in that moment that Sebastian had done it. He had killed Andrew.

"They'll put Richmont on the hunting list," Marian gasped.

"Mom...?" Jennifer stammered.

Left with no other option, Marian finally agreed to Jennifer's plan. "I'll get the spell book. But please, just let me have tonight with her. Give me tonight."

Jennifer nodded. She would cast the Forget spell on Briana tomorrow.

✳ ✳ ✳

By lunch time the next day, Briana waited in the car for Jennifer as she said 'goodbye' to her mom. Both she and Marian could feel the looming threat of an end but couldn't quite put their finger on what would happen. Thanks to magic, Jennifer had loved and lost far too many times. But from that moment on, she swore that she wouldn't let it rule her life again. Jennifer hugged her mother one last time, then climbed into her car. From her peripheral vision, she could see Marian crying on her knees. A scene she never thought she'd see. That very image brought tears to her own eyes, and she failed at her attempt to wipe them away.

"Mommy, why is grandma crying?" Briana asked from the backseat.

Jennifer turned to Briana. How the hell was she supposed to explain to her seven-year-old? She couldn't even explain it to herself.

But before she could even begin to get her words out, Briana added another question. One that hit her harder than she had ever been hit before.

"When is daddy coming back?"

Of course, Briana wasn't talking about her real father, Emerick. She was talking about Andrew. But Briana had never met Emerick. He had been another casualty in Jennifer's magical life.

Still, she mustered her courage. She had to. And she needed to be honest.

"I'm sorry, baby. But we can't see grandma anymore. And we won't be able to see daddy again, either." Those words were for Briana as much as they were for her.

But those words brought her daughter to tears, and so, Jennifer held her close.

"It's okay, baby. Mommy will take away your pain. I'll make it all better."

And that was the promise Jennifer made not only to her daughter, but also herself. That without magic in their life, they would finally be happy.

End.

Driven on her quest for female-empowerment, Reign Atkins is an Australian writer with a passion for telling action, fantasy, comedy, and Sci-Fi stories to a worldwide audience.

When not writing, Reign loves spending time with her family, playing video games, and binging on television, with a guilty pleasure for telenovelas.

For more information or to find other titles by
Reign Atkins, scan the QR below.

www.ingramcontent.com/pod-product-compliance
Lightning Source LLC
Chambersburg PA
CBHW020247120726
47904CB00001B/112